JUST MARY'S
BROWN BOOK

JUST MARY'S

BROWN BOOK

by

MARY GRANNAN

Illustrations by

PAT. PATIENCE

THOMAS ALLEN LIMITED

TORONTO

To my Sisters
ANN and HELEN

PRINTED IN ENGLAND

Contents

KAREN AND THE PIGEON

The house lights dimmed. The chatter and the rustle died down. The great audience at Pirandello's Circus sensed that the parade was about to begin. The trumpets blared and a dozen clowns tumbled to the sawdust. Ten thousand voices cheered as the dazzling spectacle unwound itself from the dark recesses of the stadium. Pirandello had surpassed himself.

The cowboys waved scarlet ten-gallon hats from the backs of their prancing palominos. The brightly colored den-wagons of the leopards were wreathed in holly. The camel, who walked haughtily on pancake feet, carried Christmas candles on his hump. Tinker, master clown of the show, cavorted behind the dignified animal, a pigeon fluttering on every finger. The people laughed at his comical antics, but the applause was thunderous when the elephants lumbered into view. Upright in the trunk of each was a small Christmas-tree dripping with baubles.

The little girl who sat alone at the rail, ringside centre, smiled happily at the passing parade. She was Karen Cardoni, small daughter of "The Flying Cardonis", the stars of the show. Although Karen had seen the parade hundreds of times, it was not until tonight that she had seen it in its new Christmas splendor. She bounced up and down in delight. With each fresh burst of approval from the audience, little Karen beamed with pride. These were her people who were being cheered. The cowboys, acrobats, equestriennes, wire-walkers, animal-trainers, bandsmen and clowns were her friends. Tinker was her favorite, of course. Tinker knew how to talk to a little circus girl, who was often lonely for playmates of her own age. She helped Tinker to clean his pigeon-cotes, and more often than once he had allowed her to handle the birds. Tinker said she had a way with pigeons.

The old clown was approaching now. He was very elegant in his oversized pantaloons of ruby satin. His cone-shaped matching cap had a sprig of mistletoe on its point. The grin on his chalk-white face widened when he saw his little friend at the rail. He flicked his forefinger, and the pigeon who perched there spread her wings and flew to Karen. The bird sank her red-booted feet into the little girl's golden curls and settled down on the child's head like a feathered bonnet.

Karen laughed. "Hello, Winnie May," she said, bending forward a little and rolling her eyes upward in an effort to see her lovely visitor. "Are you happy tonight, Winnie May? I am. Do you know something? The show closes tonight, and we're going home."

"OOah cooo-cooo-coo," said Winnie May in protest.

"Oh, but we are," said Karen. "We're going home to the farm, and I'll see my Grandmother Cardoni, and she'll kiss me on the nose to make me laugh, Winnie May, and she'll have cookies in her pantry and real strawberry jam in her cellar, but best of all she'll have a Christmas-tree in the corner for me. And I'll hang my stocking over the fireplace on Christmas Eve, and Santa Claus will come and fill it. And there'll be presents, too, under the tree. And there'll be turkey for dinner. And we'll go to the little church at the crossroads and sing Christmas hymns. I could sing one for you now, Winnie May, but the band is so loud you'd miss the lovely words about the Babe in the manger, and, besides, you'd better go back to Tinker. He'll be needing you in a little while. The parade is over. The show's going to begin."

Winnie May left the now breathless little Karen to join the clown. She wished in her pigeon heart that she could tell Karen that she was wrong. Karen

4

was not going home for Christmas. Karen was not going to hang her stocking over the fireplace or go to the little church at the crossroads. Didn't she realize that Pirandello would never dress the entire circus in Christmas colors for a one-night stand? The show was being held over. The artistry of The Flying Cardonis had been so highly praised that Pirandello felt he must satisfy the demands of the public by extending his stay in the city. Winnie May wondered why Karen had not been told.

The reason was a simple one. Lisa and Joe Cardoni risked their lives twice daily on the flying trapeze, yet they lacked the courage to tell their little daughter the disappointing news. Lisa was worried, as she stood with arms akimbo while her husband hooked the tight little bodice of her sparkling costume. "We'll have to tell her tonight, Joe," Lisa said. "We'll just have to tell her tonight." But already it was time for them to climb the rope ladder to the perch high above the centre ring.

The ring-master, who stood in the spotlight, waited until they reached the top. "Ladies and gentlemen," he called, "we give you The Flying Cardonis! Their highly hazardous feats on the flying

5

trapeze are fantastic and fabulous. Tonight Lisa Cardoni will attempt a triple somersault from the bar of her flying trapeze to the hands of her partner and husband. The Flying Cardonis!"

Karen gripped the railing as the band's slow waltz faded to a drum-roll. Her eyes never left her parents as they made ready for their perilous performance. Lisa placed an extra perch above the landing platform. Joe dusted his hands with powdered resin, set his trapeze swinging, and lowered himself into position, head downwards, his knees behind the wooden bar, his legs wrapped around the supporting ropes. Karen strained to hear the one word her mother would speak before leaping into space, but it was lost in the roll of the drums. But she did hear her father's answering "Hup". She saw her mother grasp her trapeze and swing out from the narrow platform. There was an eerie quiet in the arena as Lisa Cardoni let go, turning over and over and over. Ten thousand cries of relief echoed to the rafters as hands met wrists in a double grip.

Karen laughed aloud. They had done it again. They were safe, and now they were going home. The little girl got to her feet and started for the aisle

6

beyond. Half-way there the spotlight fell again on the ring-master. "Ladies and gentlemen, a special announcement," he called. "Because of popular demand, Pirandello's Circus will be held over for another week."

Karen stopped short in her tracks. "No, no, no," she cried. Pushing her way frantically through the milling crowd, she made her way to the dressing-room. She burst in and ran to her mother. "It's not true, Mum, is it? It's not true what the ring-master said. We are going home, aren't we? Aren't we going home?"

Still taut from the excessive strain on the trapeze, Lisa Cardoni looked with pleading eyes at her husband. He pulled Karen to him. "I'm afraid it is true, Honey," he said. "We're sorry you heard it the way you did. We should have told you before this, but we didn't have the heart."

"We'll have a good Christmas here, you'll see," Karen's mother said softly. "Be a good trouper, darling. You know the show must go on."

Karen shook her head. "I'm not a good trouper," she sobbed. "I'm not. I'm not. I don't care about the show going on. If you'd only told me, it

7

would have been alright. But now, it's too late."

"Too late for what, darling?" asked her mother, puzzled.

"For Santa Claus," came Karen's surprising answer. "I wrote him a letter. I told him I was going home. I told him I would hang my red stocking over the fireplace, and now he'll not be able to find me. Another letter couldn't reach him in time —even air-mail."

"But there must be some way to get word to him," said Joe, pacing the floor. "There must be some way to contact Santa Claus."

The door opened and in walked Tinker. He had taken off his ruby suit and conical cap, but his face was still chalk-white. He had come to borrow some cold cream to remove the grease paint. As he cleansed his face of make-up, he heard the story of Karen's predicament. For a moment he looked puzzled; then he cried triumphantly, "I have it! I know how to get a second letter to Santa Claus!"

"How?" asked the Cardonis, closing in on him.

"Winnie May, of course," said the old clown. "She's a carrier pigeon, and she'd do anything for Karen."

"I couldn't ask Winnie May to go so far, Tinker," Karen said. "Something might happen to her and, besides, you need her in your act."

Tinker snorted. "Humph," he said. "I guess you don't think much of me as an artist. I can work nine pigeons as well as ten. And as to something happening to Winnie May, another 'humph'. Old Mother Nature outfitted the pigeon in a pretty special manner. She can fly from dawn to dark, going forty, fifty, sixty and sometimes even seventy miles an hour. If we send her off in the morning, I'll bet my new red satin pantaloons she'll be back in time for the matinée on Christmas Eve."

Karen laughed. She knew how pleased Tinker was with his new pantaloons. He wouldn't risk losing them. "Oh, thank you, Tinker," she cried, "we'll do it!"

The next morning, long before the sun had thrown aside his golden blankets, Tinker and Karen were on the roof of the stadium, with Winnie May. A capsule-like letter was tucked into the metal message-holder on the pigeon's leg. "Fly in a straight line, Winnie May," Tinker whispered. "Head due north all the way until you come to the very top of the world. There you'll find Santa Claus in his castle of ice. Give him the message and wait for an answer."

"Ooah cooo-cooo-coo," said Winnie May, spreading her wings and taking flight. Karen and Tinker watched her until she became a mere speck against the dark sky of early morning.

It was an anxious day for Karen and a restless night. She dreamed that Winnie May was lost in a storm, and that she was racing across the ice-floe, calling her name. After breakfast she went to look for Tinker. She could not find him.

It was not until the afternoon matinée, when the old clown passed by her usual place by the rail, that she saw him. There was a pigeon fluttering on every finger. Winnie May had returned. With quickening heart Karen ran to "Clown Alley" to wait for Tinker. When he came in he winked at her and, reaching into the voluminous pockets of his pantaloons, he brought forth a tiny letter. "He's coming," Tinker said to the little girl. "Santa Claus is coming. It's right down here in black and white. 'Look for me tonight at the circus', and it's signed S. C."

The news soon spread among the performers that Santa Claus was coming to fill Karen's stocking. Pirandello, quick to take advantage of the unusual, called the troupe together. "We'll ask him to lead the parade," he said. "Never in the history of the circus has such a thing happened. Santa Claus and his reindeer in a circus parade!"

At eight o'clock Karen, who had been searching the sky since early evening, saw a shadow crossing the moon—a clear-cut shadow of eight tiny reindeer, a sleigh and a driver. "He's coming! He's *coming*!" she announced joyfully.

The sound of tinkling silver bells could be heard coming closer and closer. Tinker threw wide the doors, and in drove Santa Claus.

The house lights dimmed. The trumpets blared. A dozen clowns tumbled to the sawdust. Ten thousand people stood to cheer Santa Claus and the child at his side, who was wearing a pigeon for a bonnet.

(Courtesy of *Maclean's Magazine*)

LADY SILVER NOSE

She was a ship. A small ship, but she had been built with love and care in the workroom of Santa Claus. She had more than a little magic in her, too. But of this she was not aware until that Christmas Eve of the big thaw and freeze-up. Lady Silver Nose

12

had been in Santa's toy-room for many years. She had seen him come and go a dozen and one times. She had watched his red sleigh and reindeer team drive off into the night brimming over with toys while she was left behind. The years would come and the years would go, and no child would ask for an icebreaker.

"But someone must have asked me for one once upon a time, Lady Silver Nose," said the Diesel engine one day. "Santa Claus isn't one to waste his time. You're the finest icebreaker I've ever seen. Your hull is steel, and your bow could cut through ice as easily as a silver knife cuts ice-cream. I just don't understand why some little boy doesn't ask for an icebreaker."

A little boy had asked once. A little boy who lived near the Great Lakes, and who had seen ice-breakers, once wrote this letter:

"Dear Santa Claus: One day when I was driving to the city with my father I saw an icebreaker on the lakes. I'd like to have an icebreaker. My mother says that if you bring me an icebreaker she'll set a tub of water outdoors, and it will freeze and I can break the ice with my icebreaker. I hope you can bring me one, from your friend, Peter Davis."

Santa Claus had been amused by the letter. He could picture a little boy and a tub of iced water on a winter morning. He could picture the little boy setting his icebreaker into the tub and crashing through that thin top surface. Yes, Peter Davis would get his icebreaker! It took several days to make the tiny vessel, but she was a worthy ship when she was finished. Because her shining steel hull looked like silver, Santa Claus christened her "Lady Silver Nose". The old man gave the ship a final check. "Dear me," he said, "you need a bell. Any self-respecting lady of the sea needs a bell."

He couldn't find a bell in the workshop. He laughed suddenly. He left the toy-room and went to the stable. There were hundreds of tinkling silver bells on his sleigh. One would never be missed. He cut one from the shaft, shook it and said, "Little bell, you'll make the Lady Silver Nose a magic ship, but we'll not tell her she's magic. She might become a proud ship if we did. We'll give her the magic, and she'll know that she has magic powers should there ever be an hour of need. Peter Davis is getting a mighty fine gift this year."

14

But when Santa Claus went back to the house, there was another letter from Peter Davis.

"Dear Santa Claus: I am sorry to bother you with another letter, because I know you are very busy at this time of year. But, Santa Claus, something has happened. We are moving to Florida to live, and there is no ice in Florida to break, so I do not need an icebreaker. Will you, please, bring me a beach ball and a rubber horse to ride on the waves instead. From your friend, Peter Davis."

Santa Claus sighed as he put the bell on the Lady Silver Nose. "It's too bad, my lady," he said, "but you're staying home this year. Perhaps next year there'll be another Peter Davis."

But there were no more Peter Davises, and now it was Christmas-time again, and Lady Silver Nose was being left behind once again.

Every toy in the workshop, from the dolls to the electric trains, were sad of heart. They knew it must be very humiliating to go on year after year without being wanted. Susie Rag Doll decided to brighten up the toys, and she went to the toy piano and sang gaily:

"Once there was a pretty ship,
  Such a pretty gallant ship,
  With a heart of silver lining,
  And if you'll take my advice
  You will have her break your ice
  Because her hulls are steel and they are shining.
  'Cause Lady Silver Nose has a steel cap on,
  A steel cap, steel cap, steel cap on.
  'Cause Lady Silver Nose has a steel cap on,
  So very, very silver and so shining."

All the toys laughed at the funny little song that Susie Rag Doll had composed. None laughed more merrily than Lady Silver Nose. "I may not be going in Santa's sleigh," she said, "but I'm the only one who has ever had a song composed about her."

"Oh, I don't know about that," barked the little terrycloth dog. "There's a song about me. It goes like this:

  'Oh where, oh where has my little dog gone,
  Oh where, oh where can he be?
  With his tail cut short and his ears cut long
  Oh where, oh where can he be?' "

16

There was more laughter, and the fluffy little rabbit hopped forward and said, "Hah, you're not the only ones. Just listen to this. This is in all of the nursery-rhyme books:

> "*Bye lo, Baby Bunting,*
> *Daddy's gone a hunting,*
> *To fetch a little rabbit skin*
> *To wrap the baby bunting in,*
> *'Bye lo, Baby Bunting, 'bye.'*

Did you hear that? I'm mentioned in THAT song."

Others began to vie for attention. The train sang a song about his being a great big horse with a nose of iron, strong, and the velvet cat sang of the three little kittens who lost their mittens.

Santa Claus interrupted the concert. "Sorry," he said, "but it's time we were on our way."

Lady Silver Nose looked at the clock. "But it's early, Santa Claus," she said. "You never ride this early. It's still daylight."

Santa nodded his old head. "I know," he said, "but the weather is acting up. There's been a sudden thaw with a driving rain. It will be difficult for

17

the reindeer to head into such a storm, and the man at the weather bureau says the rain is going to turn to hail and that a freeze-up is following on the heels of the thaw. It's dangerous flying weather, so we'll have to start right away."

"Perhaps you could wait until after the storm, Santa Claus," said Susie Rag Doll timidly.

"I couldn't do that, Susie," Santa said. "It looks as if the storm is going to last all night. There's a little girl who's expecting to find you in her stocking tomorrow morning. We can't disappoint her and thousands of other children, can we?"

Susie Rag Doll shook her head, but her little rag heart was pounding with fear. This was to be her first ride through the sky in the reindeer sleigh, and she had been looking forward to a safe and uneventful drive. She had counted on riding among the stars and greeting the man in the moon. But tonight they would be heading into rain and sleet and hail. She moved closer to the tin soldier. He was brave, but his tin heart was pounding, too, and she knew he feared the journey as much as she did.

"Come now, come now," laughed Santa Claus, looking at his crestfallen toys. "Don't you trust me

18

to get my team through the storm? Lady Silver Nose can tell you how many storms I've faced over the years and have always come back. Do you remember ten years ago, Lady Silver Nose?"

"Yes," said the little icebreaker. "I remember it well. You couldn't see your red mitten before you when you climbed into that sleigh. I was worried all night, but you arrived back home looking like a snowman but as fresh as a daisy."

The toys felt better. They said good-bye to Lady Silver Nose, and took the places assigned to them in Santa's bags.

It was a sad little icebreaker who said "Goodbye" to Santa Claus that afternoon.

"We'll have a Merry Christmas together, Lady Silver Nose," promised the old man, "and don't worry about me. I'll turn the radio on and you'll be able to hear the weather reports. I'll probably drive out of the storm in no time." He turned on the mantel radio, and before his sleigh pulled away from the door gay Christmas music was filling the workroom.

Lady Silver Nose sighed as she thought over the long years she had been in that toy shop, unwanted by any child in the world. If Peter Davis had not moved to Florida, what a happy life she would have had breaking the ice in that tub outside his door. Her reverie was cut short by a sudden announcement on the radio.

"We interrupt our program to bring you a special announcement. A lookout man at one of our substations tells us that he saw a red sleigh and eight reindeer falling out of the sky and landing in the upper reaches of the Coppermine River. Our observer tells us that he is certain that the driver of this vehicle was Santa Claus on his way from the North Pole. The unseasonable rains opened the Coppermine directly under where the red vehicle fell. One moment, please! Another bulletin has just been handed to me. There is no doubt now that it was Santa Claus. He is safe but, as predicted, the weather has turned to freezing temperatures, and even as we speak Santa's sleigh is being sealed into the river by ice. There will be no possible way of freeing it until spring. Helicopters have already gone out to rescue Santa but it will be a sad world in the morning. Break it gently to your children, ladies and gentlemen. Tell them Santa tried, but the weather got the best of him tonight. We return to our program."

The music came on the air-waves again, but Lady Silver Nose shuddered from bow to stern. Her bell clanged and she knew for the first time that she was full of magic. Her engines began to put, put, put, put, put. She knew what she had to do. She had to free that sleigh and reindeer team from the frozen river. The enchantment of the bell made this possible. She took to the sky like a flying-boat, and in less time than you can say "Merry Christmas" she settled down on the river and, with her steel nose, she crushed the ice that was holding the sleigh as easily as you could break an egg. Telegraph wires began to buzz across the world. Radio operators were shouting out the amazing news.

"Ladies and gentlemen! Ladies and gentlemen, you won't believe this announcement, but, believe me, ladies and gentlemen, it is true. Santa Claus's sleigh and team are free from the frozen river as if by magic. An icebreaker carrying the name LADY SILVER NOSE on her stern came out of nowhere and freed the stricken sleigh. Santa Claus, refusing the aid of the helicopters that came to his rescue, has taken to the sky again, but there is no sign of the ship that cleared the way for him. She has disappeared and no one knows of her whereabouts."

Santa Claus did. Lady Silver Nose was on the seat beside him. "You have done well, Lady Silver Nose," said the old man. "I knew you would discover the magic of the bell in my hour of need."

The following Christmas Santa Claus had thousands of letters asking for an icebreaker like the Lady Silver Nose. He winked at the gallant little ship in his workroom. "I'll make icebreakers LIKE you, Lady Silver Nose," he said, "but I'll never part with you, if you don't mind."

And since the time of the sudden thaw, and the big freeze-up, the Lady Silver Nose rides proudly with Santa Claus each Christmas Eve.

THE HAPPIEST SCARECROW

The scarecrow stood sharp against the February sky. His outstretched arms were covered with new fallen snow. The brim of his black hat, which sagged over his corn-husk nose, was heavy with the starry flakes that had come in the night. The field where

23

the corn had grown tall and green in the autumn lay like an unwrinkled blanket around him. He was a lonely figure as he stood there, whipped by the winds and lashed by the storm. But he was a gallant scarecrow, always looking for a better day. He knew in his heart that up to now he had not been too successful in the work that had been assigned him. His true purpose in life was to scare crows. This he had not done. But he had tried. No one could say he hadn't tried. He had been set out in the field just as the corn began to sprout in the springtime. He had been on sentinel duty no more than an hour when the first crow had arrived.

The big black bird had circled around Mr. Scarecrow and had decided straightway that he was harmless. He peered under Mr. Scarecrow's drooping black felt hat and looked into his straw face.

Mr. Scarecrow had tried to scowl fiercely, but his scowl looked like a smile. The crow laughed. "Caw caw," he said, "you might as well give up right here and now, Mr. Scarecrow," he said. "You can't scare me. And it's not your fault, mind you. No one can blame you. You're a fine scarecrow as scarecrows go, but you're dealing with a clever bunch of birds. This time of year we travel in pairs. One of us is the lookout, to give warning in case of danger. The other does the thieving."

The scarecrow had cringed.

The crow laughed again. "You don't approve of thieves, I take it. No one does, but we can't help it. Crows are born thieves. If you ever get a chance, Mr. Scarecrow, just read what they say in the books about us. They say we rob the songbirds' nests of their eggs, that we'll steal corn and clothes-pins and silver thimbles, and even marbles. And it's all true. People admit you have to get up early to get ahead of a crow. But there's good in us, too, Mr. Scarecrow. We take the very best care of our young, and we'd fight any enemy great or small to defend them. Now you know about us, Mr. Scarecrow, if you'd like to be friends with us, we'd like to be friends with you."

Mr. Scarecrow knew that he had failed in his mission, but he decided to make the best of it. He became friends with the crows. And he enjoyed their daily visits to the cornfield. They would perch on his arm or hat, and tell him all that was going on in the world around him.

It was with dismay and sorrow that he learned in mid-November that the crows were leaving him. Some of them went south. But many of them went to the deep pine forests to spend the winter, and would not come into the open unless their food ran short.

"I'll be very lonely without you," Mr. Scarecrow said.

"Ah," said the crow, "you'll get along. You've a wide smile on your straw face, and that smile will see you through the winter. Good luck, Mr. Scarecrow, and don't let the winter winds frighten you. They're fierce and they'll blow around you and they'll bring snow and sleet, but they've good in them, too. Stand up against them. Don't let them get you down. And now, good-bye."

The smile almost left Mr. Scarecrow's straw face when he saw his last friend disappear among the pines, but he pulled himself together. "Something is sure to happen. Someone will come along," he assured himself.

Something did happen and somebody did come along.

One morning in early December, a truck rolled

26

up to the empty stone house across the road. Two men began to unload furniture. It was not long before smoke was rising out of the chimneys. It was cheerful to see smoke against the grey sky. Mr. Scarecrow watched the goings-on with great interest. At noon a car turned into the driveway. A lady and a little boy got out of it and ran into the stone house. Mr. Scarecrow's heart leapt with gladness. A little boy would be friends with a lonely scarecrow! Of that he was certain. He wondered when the little boy would discover him.

He would have been more than happy if he had known that the little boy was looking at him at the very moment he was wondering.

"Mum," the little boy said, "I love our new house and I love our new neighbor."

Mrs. Jolliffe looked at her young son, whose face was pressed against the front window. "I'm glad you like the house, Jeremy," she said, "but we've met none of the neighbors as yet. The closest one is at the next farm down the road."

"You're wrong, Mum," laughed Jeremy. "Our closest one is across the road. Look!"

"A scarecrow!" said Mrs. Jolliffe, joining in

27

Jeremy's laughter. "A fine neighbor he is! Ragged and tattered and windblown."

"I'll soon fix that," said Jeremy. "I'll brush his hat and dust his clothes, and I'll put a sprig of pine in his buttonhole. And, Mum, if you'll remember what you once told me, his clothes don't matter. You told me never to judge a person by the clothes he wore. You said it was the person inside the clothes that really mattered."

"And I meant it," said Mrs. Jolliffe. She waved her hand at Mr. Scarecrow. "Sorry, Mr. Scarecrow, I've no doubt that you're a very fine fellow indeed."

"I don't think he heard you, Mum," said Jeremy. "I'll go over and tell him, after lunch."

Jeremy was as good as his word. After lunch, and with a whisk broom, he crossed the road, climbed the fence and went into the cornfield. "Hello, Mr. Scarecrow," he said. "I'm your new neighbour, and I'm going to look after you. I'm afraid you've been neglected. Your hat needs straightening, and your clothes need brushing, and your nose is as crooked as crooked can be. My name is Jeremy Jolliffe, in case you'd like to know. Do you see that school down there by the crossroads? That's my school. I'll be

28

going there every day, and I'll tell you all that happens there because we're friends, Mr. Scarecrow."

Mr. Scarecrow had never known such happiness. Each day when Jeremy left the house he waved good morning, and each afternoon when he came back from school he climbed the fence to tell Mr. Scarecrow the happenings of the day.

Mr. Scarecrow was very proud at Christmas-time when he wore a holly wreath on the crown of his hat. The chickadees came and ate the red berries and sang carols for him.

January passed pleasantly but uneventfully. And then came February and the day of the big storm, when the field lay about Mr. Scarecrow like an unwrinkled blanket.

"I don't want you to go into the field this afternoon, Jeremy," his mother said at breakfast. "The snow is too deep. It would be away above your knees."

"But, Mum," pleaded Jeremy, "Mr. Scarecrow expects me. He has no one else to talk to him."

"You can talk to him from the fence," said his mother firmly.

"But the wind's blowing. He may not hear me,

and I want to tell him about the Valentine Party that we're going to have in school."

Mrs. Jolliffe laughed. "He'll have to make an effort to hear you, young man. You're not going into the field. Now off to school!"

The day was an exciting one for Jeremy and the other children in the class-room. Miss Pervis gave them an hour in which to draw and paint Valentines. While they were working, she made them a Valentine song. They sang it together in the afternoon.

> *"In February there's a day*
> *We send a Valentine*
> *With lacy border*
> *Doves and flowers.*
> *We say 'Will you be mine?'*
> *We offer our true loving heart*
> *And make a promise too,*
> *Come stormy weather, rain or shine*
> *To our love we'll be true."*

The children were delighted with the song. "Miss Pervis," Jeremy said, "I think we're going to have the nicest Valentine day in the world, and do you know why? We're going to have the nicest party, and we have the nicest song, and the nicest Valentine Box, and the nicest teacher."

"Thank you, Jeremy," said Miss Pervis. "I'm glad you're happy about it all."

"Oh, I am," said Jeremy. "Mr. Scarecrow will be happy too. I tell him everything. He's in the field across from our house, but Mum says I can't go into the field this afternoon. The snow is too deep. I hope Mr. Scarecrow can hear me from the fence."

The wind came up full force again in the afternoon. Jeremy had all he could do to cope with it as he made his way home. As he looked into Mr. Scarecrow's field he saw the wisdom of his mother's words. It would be folly to try to reach his friend. He waved at Mr. Scarecrow, and pointed to himself and at the drifting snow and shook his head. Then he called out, "Perhaps it will be easier to get into the field tomorrow, Mr. Scarecrow. Mr. Scarecrow, I wish you could see the lovely Valentine Box we have at school."

The wind caught up Jeremy's words and tossed them about, and all that Mr. Scarecrow heard was "Tomorrow . . . see . . . at school."

31

Mr. Scarecrow was puzzled. His straw head whirled under his black hat as he tried to figure out what Jeremy meant. Finally he came to a conclusion. "I know now what he was trying to tell me. The snow is too deep for him to walk through, but he'll see me at school tomorrow. But how can I get to the school? It's not far. I can see the school-house from here, but how can I get there for tomorrow?" He thought and thought about ways and means of getting to the school-house. He laughed suddenly. The wind would help him! He remembered what his friend the crow had said about the winds. "They're fierce," the crow had said, "but they've good in them, too." He told the wind his story and the wind was glad to lend his aid. It took the wind all of the evening and half of the night to free Mr. Scarecrow from the frozen ground. Dawn found Mr. Scarecrow on the school-house steps.

When Jeremy woke that morning he ran to the window to see how Mr. Scarecrow had weathered the storm. "Mum, Mum," he cried as he raced to the kitchen. "Mr. Scarecrow's gone. He's gone, Mum. Someone's taken my neighbor away."

"It's been the wind, darling," his mother said.

"Mr. Scarecrow just couldn't stand up against last night's blow."

Jeremy found it hard to believe his eyes when he went into the class-room that morning. Standing in the far corner, near the radiator, was Mr. Scarecrow. His mouth flew open as he stared at his friend.

Miss Pervis laughed. "He was on the doorstep this morning, Jeremy," she said. "I knew he was your Mr. Scarecrow, so I brought him inside. Do you think he'd like to be a Valentine, Jeremy? I have an old red ski suit and an old red hat with a flopping brim. We could cut out a big white heart and paint 'Will you be my Valentine' on it. He'd be the biggest and funniest Valentine in the world. What do you think, Jeremy?"

"I think he'd be very proud to be our Valentine," said Jeremy.

That afternoon Mr. Scarecrow's tattered, sodden clothes were removed, and he was dressed in the flaming red suit. The red felt hat with the floppy brim was most becoming. The children strung red hearts into garlands, and one was put in each of his hands. He looked very handsome indeed. Laughingly Miss Pervis sang:

"Oh, Mr. Scarecrow, you look fine.
Will you please be my Valentine?
You're very smart in your new clothes,
With your straw face and corn-husk nose.
We'll set you outside in the snow
Where everyone will see, and know
That we think you are very fine,
Our Mr. Scarecrow Valentine."

They set him out in the schoolyard, and people who passed by saw him and they told others. Children came from miles away to see him. He was, as Jeremy said he would be, very proud. He had failed to scare crows, but he had succeeded in making children laugh. He knew himself to be in all of the world the happiest scarecrow.

WHITE AND GREEN

Willie White was a little white rabbit, gay of heart and swift of foot. Willie had had to fend for himself almost from the day he was born. His mother's insatiable appetite for carrot greens had brought her an untimely end. She was captured in

Mr. Pennywhistle's garden. From that day on Willie's life had been one of escapes and foraging. Willie bore ill will to no one, and that's why he was amazed and more than a little unhappy when the woodland creek came up in the night and carried away his home in the briar bushes. Had not Willie leaped to a tree stump several feet away he would have been lost in the angry waters. He looked around him. The entire forest land was under water, and the water was rising every minute. He felt like a frog on a lily-pad. The situation was a new one to Willie, and he didn't know how to cope with it.

A crow, high in the pine tree, called out to him, "You'd better get out of the woodland, Willie White. The river's still flooding, and very soon that tree stump will be under water. You can make it to the hillside, Willie. Hurry, hurry, hurry."

Willie White knew good advice when he heard it. He primed his strong hind legs for the leap. With a flying jump he landed on the side of the slope. The lashing waters had muddied the hillside. Willie slipped in the muck, but with great effort managed to get his footing again. He was covered with mud from the tip of his long pink-lined ears to the tip of his powder-puff tail.

But Willie didn't mind that. Willie had gotten out of the reach of the greedy creek. He sat panting and uncomfortable on the hilltop, wondering what to do and where to go. Again the crow came to his aid. The big black bird flew to the stone pile on the hilltop and had a heart-to-heart talk with Willie.

"You might as well make up your mind, Willie, that you can't live in the woodland for quite a spell," the crow said. "Even when the water goes down, the woods won't be fit to live in. I wouldn't be surprised if it were well into June before the place dries up. You've had it hard all your life, Willie. If I were you I'd look for an easier way to live."

"Are there easier ways to live, Blackie?" asked Willie.

"Oh yes," said the crow. "There's the Zoo over at the edge of the town. There are all kinds of animals in the Zoo. Everything from elephants to field-mice! Good food is given to them. They never have to scrounge or forage. Their homes are kept clean for them, and they're treated kindly."

Willie sighed. It sounded wonderful to him.

37

Never to have to be on the alert for foxes and hawks! Never to have to break the ice and snow from the tree trunks in winter to get enough bark to survive. Blackie could see the way that Willie's mind was working, and hurriedly added, "There's just one thing about the Zoo that you should know, Willie. You'd be locked up. You couldn't go and come as you please, like you do now."

Willie's mud-covered face dropped. "It's like jail, isn't it? Like prison?" he added.

"Yes, but a very comfortable prison," said Blackie.

"Would you like it yourself, Blackie?" asked Willie White.

The big crow shook his head. "In all honesty, no," he said. "But it's different with me. I can fly. I don't have to worry about floods. My nest is out of the reach of the water, and I can always get away when I raid a farmer's garden. I'd think it over if I were you, Willie."

It was Willie's turn to shake his head. "I don't need to think it over," he said. "I know I wouldn't like being cooped up. I like my freedom. Do you have any other suggestions, Blackie?"

Blackie flapped his wings and circled the hill-top. He could think better in flight. He came back to the anxious little rabbit in a few minutes. "Of course there's always a boy," he said.

"A boy?" said Willie, puzzled.

"Yes, a boy," said the crow. "A boy loves a rabbit. A boy feeds a rabbit, looks after him, and takes him everywhere."

"Would I have my freedom if I belonged to a boy?" asked Willie, his pink eyes full of questions.

"Almost," said the crow. "Of course you'd be locked up in a hutch at night, but that would be alright. A hutch is a safe place for a rabbit. You'd have a good bed. You wouldn't mind the hutch. Yes, Willie, I think if I were you I'd look for a boy."

"Do you suppose a boy would want me?" said Willie, wriggling now to free himself of the mud. It was beginning to dry and tighten.

Blackie assured Willie that somewhere there was a boy who wanted a rabbit.

Neither of them knew that such a boy lived in the red-brick house on the corner of Daffodil and Magnolia Streets. At the moment the little boy was restless. He was practising his music lesson. After

39

working at his scales for too short a time he called pleadingly, "Mum, will that do for today?"

"It certainly will not do for today," said the little boy's mother. "You know you've done hardly any work this week."

Peter sighed and turned again to his exercises. After considerable effort, he decided that he would sing a song of Easter. Peter knew the real meaning of Easter, but his song was not of that but of an Easter gift that he hoped to receive. A rabbit! Peter wished for a rabbit with all his heart. He put his own words to a simple tune that he could play.

"I hope that at Easter-time
A small rabbit will be mine.
He will be as white as snow,
He will like me, that I know.
I will be both good and kind
To the rabbit, who is mine."

Mrs. Green smiled as she went about her work in the kitchen. She heard the song, and knew that Peter meant every word he sang. "That will do, dear," she called. "Come to the kitchen now. I've a surprise for you."

Peter, glad to be free of his musical task, lost no time in reaching his mother's side. "I heard your song," Mrs. Green said. "You want a rabbit very much, don't you, Peter?"

"Oh yes, Mum, a white rabbit," said Peter. "I think every boy should have a real rabbit at Easter. Chocolate rabbits are nice, but I'd rather have a real one."

Peter cried out happily when his mother gave him fifty cents and told him to go to the market and get his rabbit. "They're sure to have rabbits at the market at this time of year," she said. "Every little boy seems to want one at Easter."

Peter nodded excitedly as he thanked his mother, and set out to make his wish come true.

As Peter Green was trudging down the street, Willie White was trudging up the highway and toward town. The crow had told him that he would find a boy in town. When he reached the crossroads Willie White saw a big billboard. He stopped to stare up at it. There was a picture of a white rabbit on the board. The rabbit was standing on his hind legs, pointing toward the city with one chubby paw as if directing traffic. Willie White laughed and waved. "I'm going that way," he said. And then he read the words on the billboard. "Easter Bunnies for sale at King Street Market."

Forgetting how muddied he was from his recent experience in the woodland, Willie White hopped forward with new vigour. Now he knew exactly where to go to find a boy. The market!

But when he reached the market he could not get in. He was blocked at every entrance. "Shoo, go away, you muddy little bunny. Go away! Everything is clean in here. We can't let you into the market. Shoo . . . shoo . . . off with you."

It was at the south door that Willie White gave up. He sat down on the curb panting with disappointment. If he could have made himself heard he could have told the people that under his muddy coat he was the whitest, fluffiest bunny in the world. But there was such a din. There was the chatter of the customers. The cries of the vendors. "Fresh eggs, fresh eggs, get your fresh eggs here! Flowers! Flowers! All kinds of flowers. They'll bring you many happy hours. We've daffodils, tulips and hyacinths blue. Get your fresh flowers, we've all kinds for you."

It was hopeless to make himself heard, and he sat there despondently, wondering what to do next.

Willie White was not the only unhappy one at the market. Peter Green was unhappy, too. He had arrived too late to get a rabbit. As he walked from stall to stall he got the same answer. "No rabbits. We're sold out. There's a great demand for rabbits at Easter-time. No rabbits! No rabbits!"

Disheartened, Peter Green went out the south door of the market and sat down on the curb, beside Willie White. He didn't notice Willie. Willie was so muddy he matched the pavement. But Willie White saw Peter Green. "Hello, little boy," he said eagerly.

"Hello, little brown rabbit," said Peter, turning to look at the little fellow at his side.

"I'm not brown," said Willie. "I'm white. Willie White! I got caught in the flooding waters and I slipped into the mud. But I'm as white as snow underneath, and I'm looking for a boy."

Peter picked up the mud-caked Willie and held him close. "You've found a boy, Willie White. Come on, let's go home."

Peter's mother was aghast when she saw Willie. "Peter," she cried, "where on earth did you get that

43

filthy rabbit? You didn't buy him, surely?"

"No, I didn't buy him, Mum," said Peter, "but he's mine. He was looking for a boy, Mum, and he found me. He's as white as snow underneath. May I have your scrubbing-brush and some laundry soap, please?"

A half-hour later Willie White was white again, and fluffy and beautiful. The next day Willie White and Peter Green went in search of Blackie the Crow. They wanted to thank him and to wish him a Happy Easter.

URSULA'S SHAWL

Have you ever wondered about the rainbow?
Some think it is a bridge for the angels. Some think
it is a giant bow, and that the lightning flashes are its
arrows. Others think it is a fairy roadway. But I
think it is Ursula's shawl, and Ursula is the Great
Bear of the sky.

It was spring, and all things were fresh and new. The rivers, free of winter ice, were laughing their way to the sea. Earth was emptying her dark brown pockets. Flowers were blooming everywhere. And the bluebird sang:

> "Spring is here! Spring has come.
> Every heart is glad and gay.
> Flowers bloom, streamlets sing,
> And the robin's here to stay.
> Sunshine's bright! Sunshine's warm!
> And the sky is clear and blue.
> Everyone is happy, and
> Ladies wear their bonnets new."

But Ursula, the Great Bear in the sky, looked on the fresh world and the new bonnets and was sad. There was no spring in her life. She had no new bonnet, and she wanted one. She turned her bright eyes from the woodland, where the bluebird sang and the rivers laughed, and looked on the scurrying people in the cities. She saw new bonnets everywhere. They were bedecked with flowers and gay with ribbons. Some had feathers perched on their crowns, and all were beautiful. Ursula wanted an Easter bonnet. Her yearning became so great that her light dulled. The other stars noticed this and were fearful.

"She is worried about something," said Cygnus, the swan.

"But what has she to worry about?" asked Draco, the dragon. "She is one of the most popular stars in the sky, and the children down on the earth love her. They are always pointing her out. I have heard them say many times, 'There is the Great Bear and the Little Bear'. They never look at me. They never point to Draco, the dragon. I don't think she's worried."

Jupiter shook his starry head. "Why don't we ask her what's troubling her instead of guessing among ourselves. It might be that we could help her."

"You are right, Jupiter," said Dolphin, the fish star. "She respects your opinions. You ask her."

Jupiter went to Ursula. But Ursula assured Jupiter there was nothing wrong. She was really ashamed of herself for wanting an Easter bonnet. She could imagine their laughter if they knew.

"Ursula in a bonnet! The Great Bear wearing a hat!" The whole world would be for ever laughing!

So Ursula kept her secret pent up within her, and grew duller as the days went by. Finally the Little Bear knew he must do something. He went to his mother. "Mama," he said, "you have told Jupiter that nothing is wrong, but something must be wrong. I know, because I am your child. You can trust me with your secret. Please tell me, Mama."

Ursula nodded her starry head. "I know I can trust you, my child, and I know I shall feel better if I get my silly secret out of my heart. Little Bear, I have been looking down on the earth people; and I can see that it is spring down there, when everything is fresh and new, and all the ladies are wearing new bonnets. I want an Easter bonnet."

The Little Bear gasped. His mother in an Easter bonnet! But he wanted to help her, and although getting her an Easter bonnet seemed almost too much to cope with, he made up his mind to try.

That night he slid to earth on a moonbeam, and landed right in the path of a little white rabbit who had been scampering about in the moonlight. "You frightened me, Little Bear," the rabbit said. "I didn't see you coming. It was just as if you had dropped out of the sky."

"I did," said the Little Bear.

"You did what?" asked the rabbit.

"I did drop out of the sky. I slid to earth on a moonbeam. I am the sky's Little Bear."

The rabbit laughed. He thought the Little Bear was joking, but when he saw the stardust in the bear's fur he realized it was true. "Why are you here?" he asked. "Why did you leave the sky? I like you up there. I like the Big Bear, too."

"She is my mother," said the Little Bear. "And I came down here because she is unhappy."

The rabbit shook his head sympathetically. "That is too bad. It is the spring-time, when everything is new and everyone should be happy."

Little Bear nodded. "But that is why she is unhappy." The rabbit looked puzzled. "I mean," went on the Little Bear, "that she has seen all the freshness on earth and all the ladies in their new bonnets." The Little Bear laughed half-heartedly. "I might as well tell you. My mother wants an Easter bonnet."

The rabbit bit his lip quickly to keep from

laughing, but the Little Bear knew the effort he was making to keep back his merriment. "Go ahead and laugh," he said. "I don't mind. I almost laughed myself. I know she shouldn't wear an Easter bonnet on her big head, but I do want her to be happy again so that she will twinkle for you little rabbits and for all the earth people."

The rabbit sat down on a tree stump and pondered. He wanted to help the little sky Bear, who was so concerned about his mother's happiness. "Perhaps," he said, "we might be able to find a hat in the city that is large enough. Let's go and look into the hat-shop windows."

Together they trotted off side by side in the starlit night, and made their way to the city. The streets were deserted. Even the policeman making his nightly rounds had left the main street. The hat hunters soon found a millinery shop, and stopped to stare into the window. There were large hats, which were the height of fashion on that night so long ago, but both the rabbit and the Little Bear knew that they were most unsuitable for the Great Bear in the sky.

The little rabbit shook his head, and they both

left the window and went slowly down the street. Then suddenly the rabbit stopped and pointed with his white paw to another show window which was filled with beautiful shawls. "Don't you think your mother would be just as happy with a beautiful shawl? You can see they are all in the fashion."

"Yes," said the Little Bear. "A beautiful shawl of many colors would add beauty to the sky, too. We shall get a shawl for her."

They sat down together to think of the most beautiful colors in the world. "Red," said the little rabbit quickly. "Red like geraniums."

"Orange," said the Bear. "Orange like marigolds."

"Yellow," laughed the rabbit. "Yellow like the daffodils."

"Green," almost shouted the Little Bear. "Green like the grass and the leaves and the mosses."

"Blue," cried the rabbit. "Blue like the delphiniums that grow tall in the garden."

"Violet," said the Little Bear very softly. "Violet like the violets that grow in your own deep woods, velvety and fragrant and beautiful. Let us get the shawl right away!"

51

The Little Bear was so excited that he was twinkling all over the place. The street was as bright as day. The little rabbit cried out, "Calm down! Calm down! You'll wake up the people. You're making things so bright they'll think it is morning. Calm down and listen. We can't get the shawl right away. Shawls like that don't grow on trees, you know. It will have to be made. We shall have to get help. It will be a gossamer shawl."

It was the Little Bear's turn to look puzzled. "Cobwebs," said the little rabbit. "We'll find a big meadow, and all the spiders in it will spin gossamer until the meadow is carpeted with it. Then we shall get the flowers to stripe it with their colors. The birds will carry it up to the sky. We have no time to waste. Come on, we must talk with Great-grandmother Spider. If she says yes, the other spiders will do the same."

The old spider listened to the eager little two with great interest. "It would be a great undertaking, of course, to make a gossamer that would stretch across the sky," she said. "I'm sure we could do it if we worked together, but we have our pride, you know. We would want the world to see our work. If you will let me name a time when the whole world may see our work, I will give the order to go ahead."

The Little Bear looked at the rabbit. The rabbit nodded. "We agree to that, Grandmother Spider. When would you like your gossamer to be seen by the world?"

"At an unusual and beautiful time. Let me think. Our webs appear as shining silver when the sun shines on them after a shower. That is the time I choose. When the sun comes out during a shower, the world will see our beautiful gossamer stretching across the sky."

The little rabbit hopped up and down in glee. "We'll call the gossamer Ursula's shawl, Grandmother Spider. What a lovely name. Ursula's shawl!"

The great task was begun. The birds asked the flowers to color the gossamer, and the flowers came silently in the night from the woods and gardens, the fields and greenhouses, leaving a trail of red, orange, yellow, green, blue and violet over the filmy silken shawl. The spiders worked tirelessly on the web. Old Great-grandmother Spider sang:

53

"Spin and spin the gossamer shawl;
Spin and spin the colors so bright.
Blue and yellow, violet and green,
And red from the geraniums bright.
And orange like gold
From the marigold,
Are woven into the gossamer light.

"When the Great Bear's fine shawl is finished,
Orioles and tanagers, too.
Robins, bluebirds, sparrows and blackwings
Will go flying into the blue.
They'll carry with care
The gossamer there,
They'll carry it there to Ursula Bear."

And on and on spun the spiders until the shawl was finished. The bluebirds and the robins, the orioles and the scarlet tanagers, carried it to the sky, and draped it over the shoulders of Ursula the Great Bear in the sky. She was very pleased with her Easter gift, and wore her shawl proudly. The Little Bear climbed home on a moonbeam.

It was many days before the rain and the sun

came together, but when they did the sky was aglow with colors. The little rabbit, the spiders and the birds cried out with delight at the result of their joint effort. And the people on that long-ago day cried out, too, in awe and wonder. "Look! Look into the sky! A bridge of color!"

"It must be for angels," said one.

"It may be a fairy roadway," suggested another.

"It looks like a giant bow to me," said a third. "It came with the rain. I am going to call it a rainbow." And from that day it has been called a rainbow.

They did not know it was Ursula's shawl. How could they know? But you know, and I know, and I believe. Do you?

MR. PEABODY'S THINKING-CAP

It was a very ordinary cap, made of very ordinary flecked tweed. It had a wide peak on the front and a button on the middle of the top. It was quite threadbare, and although Mr. Peabody had other caps and hats, he could never quite bring himself to throw it away. It hung on a nail in his workshop, where Mr. Peabody puttered about many happy hours each day. Mr. Peabody was old. He had retired and had time to putter. He had time also for little Debbie Dooley, who lived next door. It was no trouble at all for Mr. Peabody to mend a broken wagon or doll or to answer any question. One morning Debbie went into his shop with a question that really puzzled Mr. Peabody.

"Mr. Peabody," Debbie said, "last night, before I went to sleep, I was looking into the sky and, Mr. Peabody, would you believe it, a star fell? I saw it, Mr. Peabody. I saw it with my own eyes. It was up there silver and twinkling, and all of a sudden it fell. I thought it fell into our garden, and this morning I looked for it; but it wasn't there, and it's not in your garden either, and now I know it didn't fall all the way. I think it just dropped a little. Mr. Peabody, what do you think happened to that star? Why did it fall?"

Mr. Peabody rubbed his chin with his thumb and forefinger. Then he scratched his head. Then he took off his glasses, polished them with his handkerchief and put them on again. Debbie waited patiently. Debbie knew that Mr. Peabody always went through those motions when he was thinking deeply, and usually by the time his glasses were back on his nose he had the answer. But today he shook his head. Then he looked at the cap on the nail. "Just a minute, Debbie, I'll put on my thinking-cap."

He reached for the cap. He set it on top of his silver curls, and a wide smile spread over his face and his eyes twinkled like the star that had fallen.

Debbie tugged at his coat sleeve. "Did it tell you, Mr. Peabody? Did your thinking-cap tell you why the star fell?"

Mr. Peabody nodded and sang:

"I heard a strange story from this cap of mine,
It sang to me of that old Mother Goose rhyme;
Of the cat and the fiddle,
The dish and the spoon,
And the cow who went jumping
Right over the moon.
And last night she jumped o'er
The moon once again.
She kicked a small star and it fell, and
'*Twas then,*

*'Twas then that you saw it fall down in the
sky.
The jumping cow kicked it when she jumped
so high."*

Debbie laughed and laughed. So did Mr.
Peabody. Neither of them had suspected that the
thinking-cap would tell them such a funny story.
When Debbie recovered from her laughter, she looked
at the cap closely and then at Mr. Peabody.

"Mr. Peabody," she said, "I've seen that old
cap hanging on the nail every day, but I didn't even
dream it was a thinking-cap. Can it answer all our
questions, sir?"

Mr. Peabody wasn't too sure about that. He
rubbed his chin, scratched his head and polished his
glasses again. "We shouldn't overwork the old
thinking-cap," he said. "If it answers one question a
day, I think it's all we should expect."

Debbie agreed that they shouldn't overwork the
thinking-cap. It was too precious to overwork.
Now that they'd discovered the magic in the cap,
they must guard their treasure carefully.

It was two days later that Debbie came racing to

the workshop. She was carrying with her a small wooden horse. The horse was red and splotched with yellow. Its mane and tail drooped wearily. "Mr. Peabody," said Debbie, setting the horse on the workbench, "there's something wrong with my horse. He's not happy today. His tail is all saggy and his mane is all draggy, and when I went for him this morning there were tears in his eyes."

Mr. Peabody bit his lip to keep from smiling. "Didn't I see him on the back step this morning?" he asked.

"Yes, sir," said Debbie. "That's where I left him yesterday."

"Um," said Mr. Peabody. "It rained in the night. Don't you think that the tear you saw might have been a raindrop, and don't you think that the rain might have something to do with the saggy mane and the draggy tail?"

Debbie shook her head violently. "No, sir," she said. "I don't. It was a real teardrop. I can tell teardrops from raindrops."

Mr. Peabody reached for his thinking-cap. What else could he do? If Debbie were sure it was a teardrop, how else could they find out the reason for the

sad state of the little horse? He set the cap on top
of his silver curls, and, although he smiled, the smile
was a puzzled one. "Doesn't it tell you, Mr. Peabody," asked Debbie. "Doesn't it tell you?"

"It tells me and it doesn't tell me," said the old
man. "What do you suppose my thinking-cap says?"

Debbie shook her head. She had no idea what
the thinking-cap had told Mr. Peabody.

Once again Mr. Peabody sang the thinking-cap's
message:

> *"If you want to find*
> *Why the horse is sad,*
> *If you want to find*
> *Why it is not glad,*
> *Take it to the Fair,*
> *And take Debbie, too.*
> *At the Fair you will learn the reason."*

Debbie hopped up and down in delight. Although she was sorry for her little wooden horse
with the saggy mane and the draggy tail, she was glad
that they had to go to the Fair to learn why he had a
tear in his eye. "First, I'll have to ask Mum if I may

61

go to the Fair. I think she'll say 'yes'. I'll be right back, Mr. Peabody, and, Mr. Peabody, don't forget to take your thinking-cap with you. We may need it."

Mrs. Dooley laughed merrily when she heard about the sad horse. "But, darling," she said, "aren't you just pretending? You don't want to drag poor Mr. Peabody away from his workbench, do you?"

"He wants to go, Mum," said Debbie. "He always does what his thinking-cap tells him, and the thinking-cap told him that we'd find out why my horse was sad at the Fair."

Mrs. Dooley agreed that under the circumstances Debbie should go to the Fair. She helped Debbie to change into a fresh dress, and gave her fifty cents to spend. And off went Debbie and Mr. Peabody. She was carrying the sad horse. He was carrying the thinking-cap.

As they neared the Fair grounds they could hear gay music. They could hear the cries of the vendors. "Balloons, balloons! Get your balloons! Step up, step up, everybody play ball. Hurry, hurry, hurry, see the performing monkeys direct from the jungles of South America."

Debbie was almost dancing, she was so excited.

Mr. Peabody said that he thought they should see the monkeys and the elephants and the dog show before he put on his thinking-cap. He said that he was quite sure the little wooden horse wouldn't mind if they took time out for some pleasure and some ice-cream. After they had seen almost everything that was to be seen, and after they'd heard almost everything that was to be heard, Debbie looked up at her good friend. He nodded. He put on his thinking-cap and he nodded again. He took Debbie's hand and led her toward the Merry-go-round. "It has something to do with the Merry-go-round," he said. "I'm not quite sure what it is, but if we ride on a horse, with the horse, we'll find out. Come on, let's go."

Once again Debbie was delighted at the way things were working out. She had wanted to ride on the Merry-go-round, but her mother had told her not to make any suggestions to Mr. Peabody. She had done as her mother had told her, and things were working out very well indeed. She was surprised at the way Mr. Peabody mounted the galloping golden horse on the Merry-go-round. Somehow she had never thought of Mr. Peabody riding on a Merry-go-round. He looked very jolly on the saddle, his thinking-cap still nestling on the silver curls. The calliope began to play and Mr. Peabody began to sing :

"I know now why your horse is sad,
He wants to be on the Merry-go-round.
He's too small to carry the children,
That's why he was crying, I've found.
He wants to go 'round on the Merry-go-round,
He wants to go 'round,
And 'round and around."

After the ride and the discovery of why Debbie's little horse was sad, the little girl and the old man walked home together. "I wouldn't worry about it, Debbie," the old man said. "He'll get over it. He's had one nice ride on the Merry-go-round. Perhaps that will perk him up."

Debbie sighed. "But it didn't," she said. "Look, sir, his tail is still saggy and his mane is still draggy. But he must try to forget the whole idea. There's no way that he can be a Merry-go-round horse."

Mr. Peabody said he wasn't so sure about that. "Of course I know he couldn't be on a big Merry-go-round, but there might be a way he could go around and around. We can't use the thinking-cap again until tomorrow. We both promised that we'd not overwork the thinking-cap. Come over in the morning, Debbie, and I'll put it on and we'll see what happens. Bring the horse with you, just in case."

Mr. Peabody had the thinking-cap in his hand when Debbie went to his workshop the next morning. He put it on and he laughed. "It is all so simple," he said. "So very simple. Debbie, you have a big spinning-top, haven't you?"

"Yes, sir," said Debbie.

"Get it. My thinking-cap told me that if I fastened the little horse to the top of the spinning-top and balanced him just right, he can go around and around and around as much as he likes."

The little horse did, and there were no more tears in his eyes. But, strangely, his mane was still draggy and his tail was still saggy. But as Debbie said, "You can't have everything."

And that's the story of Mr. Peabody's thinking-cap—a very ordinary cap to look at, but as full of enchantment as a fairy-ring when the moon is low.

MANDY MONDAY

Mandy liked her name. People always smiled
when they heard it. "But is that really your name?"
they would ask. "Is your name really Mandy
Monday?"

And Mandy would hop about on one foot
chanting:

"Mandy Monday, Mandy Monday
Named Amanda, and born on Sunday."

Mandy was never called Amanda. It didn't seem right for such a merry little blue-eyed girl to be called Amanda. Mandy suited her, and Mandy it was. Mandy had the danciest feet in the world. They didn't like to stay in one place. They carried her up street and down, over meadows and across and round corners. Mandy Monday's dancing feet loved to go round corners. But they always stopped at Miss Hetty Huckleberry's sweet shop.

Mandy mentioned this one day when the sun was shining. "It's a funny thing, Miss Hetty Huckleberry," she said, "but my feet always stop outside your door. They run up the street and down, over the meadows and across, but just as soon as I round the corner where your sweet shop is they stop. Do you know the reason, Miss Hetty Huckleberry?"

The little old lady behind the snowy-white counter nodded an equally snowy-white head. "I've been waiting for you to ask me that, Mandy Monday," she said. "I was hoping you would. I couldn't do a thing until you did ask."

67

Mandy's blue eyes widened as she looked up at Miss Hetty. "I don't know what you mean," she said. "I would have asked before if I'd known you were waiting, Miss Hetty Huckleberry."

Miss Hetty moved the sliding door of the candy case, took out a violet-colored confection and set it on the counter. "Would you care for a sweet while we talk over the matter, Mandy?"

Mandy nodded. "Thank you," she said. "How did you know it was my day for sweets? My mother lets me have candy once a week. And this is my day. Too much candy is not good for my teeth, you know, and you can't smile if you have poor teeth, and I like smiling."

She sank her white teeth into the sparkling violet cream, and sat down on one of the little white chairs in the shop to wait for Miss Hetty Huckleberry to speak.

The little old lady's eyes were twinkling as she came from behind the counter to sit with Mandy. "You and I, Mandy Monday, have a magic bond between us. We have unusual names. Yours has two 'M's'. Mine has two 'H's'. That's what makes the magic bond. That is why your dancing feet stop at my door."

"Is it?" said the amazed Mandy. "And I always thought it was because you gave me a sweet when my feet stopped."

"Oh no. It's the magic. With a name like yours, you can go magic places," said Miss Huckleberry, nodding mysteriously.

"Can you go magic places, Miss Huckleberry, too?" asked Mandy.

"Not now. But I used to go when I was your age," said Miss Hetty. "One grows out of magic, you know. But you are still in the magic circle because of the two 'M's'. Those two 'M's' can take you any-where."

Mandy was so excited about the prospects that lay ahead that she popped the rest of the sweet into her mouth and gulped it down. "Where did your two 'H's' take you, Miss Huckleberry?"

Miss Huckleberry pondered the question. "It's been such a long time," she said. "I need a minute to think."

Mandy waited almost breathlessly. She was relieved when Miss Huckleberry smiled widely. "I remember once, a day in spring it was, when the birds were coming back from the south. I met a

69

bluebird in the meadow by the river and I said to him, 'Good morning, Mr. Bluebird, I'm glad you have come back to sing for us. My name is Hetty Huckleberry, and how are you?' To my great surprise, he said, 'I'm fine, Hetty Huckleberry. I'm glad you spoke to me. You've two "H's" in your name and I've two "B's". There's a magic bond between us. Where would you like to go?' And I said, 'I'd like to see the land behind the stars.' And would you believe it? He took me there. And although I was a little girl just the size of you, Mandy Monday, I flew away on that bluebird's back, above the tree-tops and church steeples, to the Land of the Stars, and when I got there the stars sang to me."

"What did they sing, Miss Huckleberry? What did they sing?" cried the delighted Mandy Monday.

"At first I heard them twinkle," said Miss Huckleberry, "and then they sang:

> *'Miss Hetty Huckleberry,*
> *We are so very*
> *Glad that you flew*
> *Up through the blue.*

70

Miss Hetty, Miss Hetty,
We wish you gladness
All your life through,
All your life through.' "

Miss Hetty clasped her hands together, and looked at Mandy as if she were wishing that she could bring back the magic days. Mandy laughed. Mandy had ideas. She was going to travel, too. "I'm going some place, too, Miss Huckleberry," she said. "I'm going some place, but I don't know where; and thank you for telling me about the magic of Mandy Monday."

Miss Hetty held up a restraining hand. "Wait, Mandy. There is one thing I didn't tell you. You must meet something or somebody with two letters the same. You will remember I went with bluebird. Two 'B's'! I also had an adventure with a fluffy fox. Two 'F's'! Another day I went floating off with a silver snowflake. Two 'S's'. Be sure to look for two letters the same."

"I shall, Miss Huckleberry, and I'll come back to tell you of my magic adventure."

Mandy Monday left the shop, and her feet began to dance again. The first one she met was a little red-

71

booted pigeon who had stopped to peck for seeds. The pigeon was gray. "Gray pigeon," said Mandy, and shook her head. She went skipping across the meadow (the same meadow in which Miss Huckleberry had met her bluebird long, long ago), and she met a rabbit. It was white. White Rabbit! It was not magic. The search continued for some time without success.

She sat down on the river bank. A shingle came floating downstream, like a tiny ship without sails. Mandy saw it and said to herself, "I wonder where that shingle ship came from." She leaped to her feet. A shingle ship! Two "S's". It was magic. Mandy called out. "Hello, Shingle Ship. My name is Mandy Monday. Where are you going?"

The little shingle ship began to sing:

"I am a-sailing far off to the sea,
Mandy Monday, Mandy Monday.
Mandy, would you like to sail off with me?
To sail far off to sea?
We'll ride the sea-foam,
And then come back home.
Would you like to sail with me?"

Mandy's answer was to run down the bank. Like Miss Huckleberry's bluebird, the shingle had grown in size. It was big enough when Mandy reached it to sit on comfortably. Mandy climbed aboard, and sang in answer:

"I'd love to go sailing far off to the sea!
Over the sea! Over the sea!
I am so happy that you're taking me
Over the big blue sea.
Set sail, let us go;
We'll have fun, I know,
Out on the big, big sea."

And down the river they sailed, the two "M's" and the two "S's", and everyone who saw them called out in amazement, "Look! Look! There goes Mandy Monday on a shingle ship."

They sailed past villages and towns, and wharfs and docks, and big sailing vessels and little sailing vessels, and cargo ships and pleasure ships. On and on they went together. Mandy Monday thought that it would be all clear sailing. The thought of danger didn't occur to her. She didn't consider for a moment that her magic craft was frail. When they

73

reached the mouth of the river, where it poured its waters into the ocean, the currents grew stronger. They were tossed about on the breakers. Up they went and over the big waves, and on and on, out to the open sea. Mandy suddenly realized that although the shingle ship was riding the waves very well, it was growing smaller. With each lashing wave a splinter or two broke away.

"I think," Mandy said to the ship, "that we'd better go home."

"I think so, too," said the shingle. "I feel my sides splitting. We should have stayed in the river, Mandy. The ocean is too much for me."

Suddenly they heard a great deep voice echoing over the waves, and they heard someone singing. They listened.

> *"I am a great big whopping whale,*
> *And my name it is Whopper.*
> *I swim about in the deep sea*
> *And I splash up the water.*
> *Whopper, Whopper, Whopper Whale,*
> *Whopper splashes water.*
> *I am a great big Whopping Whale,*
> *And my name it is Whopper."*

74

Mandy clasped her hands and laughed. "Whopper Whale! Two 'W's'." She called out to the whale and told him of her predicament. "Climb aboard my back, Mandy Monday, and bring your ship with you."

Mandy climbed aboard the broad back of the great sea creature and pulled the shingle aboard. The whale shook his giant head. "I'm afraid I'm too big to go into the shallow waters of the river to take you home," he said. "Whales never go into rivers. But I think I have an idea. I'll call Silas Seahorse. He's a very obliging little steed. He'll take you home. Silas! Silas!"

A little seahorse came galloping through the waves, toward the whale and Mandy. "You calling me, Whopper?" he neighed. He looked at Mandy and the shingle ship. "Oh, you've visitors."

"Yes, Silas, and they're stranded," said Whopper. "The ship is not seaworthy, and they want to go home. They live up-river. Will you take them there, Silas?"

Silas Seahorse looked at Mandy. "What's your name?" he asked.

"Mandy Monday," the little girl said.

"It's alright. You have two 'M's'. Can you ride

75

bareback? I've no saddle, you know," said Silas.

Mandy was sure that she could ride bareback. She climbed from the whale to the back of the sea-horse and, clasping the shingle ship in her arms, she announced that she was ready to go. "Thank you very much, Whopper," she said to the whale. "I don't know what we would have done without you."

Mandy enjoyed the trip back to the river's mouth and up-stream. The little seahorse cantered along at an easy pace, and it was no time at all before she was in the meadow again. She ran to the sweet shop and Miss Hetty Huckleberry. Miss Hetty could tell immediately that Mandy had had an adventure. "What did you find that was magic?" she asked Mandy. "A bluebird? A robin redbreast? A green goblin?"

"None of those things," said Mandy. "A shingle ship! We went sailing off to sea; but the shingle wasn't seaworthy, and we were in great danger, and then Whopper Whale came along, and we sat on his back, and he called Silas Seahorse, who brought us home. I didn't expect to run into danger, Miss Huckleberry. I didn't know there was danger in magic."

76

"Of course there is," said the little shopkeeper. "Do you forget the danger that Jack met when he climbed up the beanstalk? And the danger Red Riding Hood ran into when she met the wolf, and Hansel and Gretel when they met the old woman of the wood? But, of course, all of the stories turned out happily in the end, just as yours did." Miss Huckleberry slid the door of her candy case again, and set a pink bon-bon on the counter. "After all you've been through, I think you should eat this to strengthen you, Mandy Monday."

Mandy agreed. "One more won't hurt my teeth," she said, "and I do need it to strengthen me."

Miss Huckleberry laughed merrily as the little girl went down the street and round the corner. It was nice to have dancing feet and a name like Mandy Monday.

LITTLE GOOD ARROW

A night-hawk screeched. His harsh notes echoed and echoed again across the deep lake in the forest. A loon laughed. The little Indian who sat by the water's edge looked upward. He could see the white breast of the grey bird against the darkening

sky of evening. He watched as the loon, face to the
wind, slanted downward, striking the top of a tower-
ing wave with the lightness of a birch canoe. The
little Indian knew why he came. The little Indian
had seen the loon's nest on the ground close to the
water's edge. He had seen two dark green eggs in the
nest. The loon laughed again . . . wildly . . . taunt-
ingly.

The little Indian cried out, "Stop it! Stop
laughing at me. I know why you're laughing. I
know why. It's because of my name. Everyone
laughs at my name."

The bird turned his head shoreward, and looked
at the unhappy little Indian who had interrupted his
eerie chant to the evening. He saw a small boy in
buckskin. His moccasined feet dangled over the rock
on which he was sitting. What did the little Indian
mean? He was not laughing at his name, whatever
his name might be. He was announcing the coming
of an easterly gale. If the little Indian were wise he
would go to his wigwam.

There was a rustle among the bushes along the
bank. An old Indian woman, wrinkled with the sun
and wind of many summers, stepped into the clear-

ing. "Here you are, my little one," she said. "Your father, the great chief, has been looking for you. He is worried. A storm is approaching. Did you not hear the loon's warning?"

"He was laughing at me," sobbed the little Indian.

The old one put her arms about the weeping child. "And why should he laugh at you, my sweet one?" she asked. "You are strong and handsome, and I, your grandmother, am very proud of you, Little Nothing Yet."

"That's why he was laughing. That's why. My name! 'Little Nothing Yet'! Why does everyone call me 'Little Nothing Yet'?"

The old one took his hand. "I did not know the name troubled you. It is not meant unkindly. It is just that you are young and have done nothing yet."

A flash of lightning cut across the sky. Thunder rolled angrily in its wake. "Come, we must hurry before the rain. I shall speak to your father, the great chief, about your unhappiness."

Little Nothing Yet's answer was lost in the fury of the oncoming storm. He hurriedly followed his grandmother to the encampment and the warmth of her teepee. He was soon fast asleep.

When the storm lessened the old one went to her son, the great chief of the tribe. "Your little one has a heavy heart," she said.

The great chief frowned. He was puzzled. "Why should he be heavy of heart?" he asked. "I give him all the love I have in me. You have raised him as kindly and tenderly as his mother, who is with the Great Spirit, would have done. Where have we failed, my mother?"

The old one smiled slowly. "We have not failed. We have made a mistake. We have belittled him."

"Belittled him!" repeated the chief. "In what way?"

"In calling him 'Little Nothing Yet'," said the old lady. "We have called him that in endearment, to be true, but it has been thoughtless of us. Children have pride, you know. Children need to feel important. They need to feel that they are people who have a place in the world. When you think it over, my son, the name 'NOTHING YET' is a hard one to carry about. How could our little one feel important with such a name?"

The chief nodded. "We have been thoughtless.

81

Every time he hears the name it is probably like an arrow in his heart. I shall talk to him in the morning. I shall tell him to make a name for himself."

And, in the morning, Little Nothing Yet was summoned by his father, the great chief. "I have talked with your grandmother, my son. I have learned of your sadness, and I think it is time that you made a name for yourself."

The small boy's dark eyes widened. "But I do not know how to do that, my father."

The great chief smiled. "We shall talk it over," he said. "There are many ways to win a name. Strong Bow of our tribe is so called because he has a strong arm with his bow. Light Foot won his name because he runs swiftly and far with great ease. Young Chief Great Bear earned his name early in life when he brought to my teepee the great bear on whose skin you are now standing. Perhaps you might like to be a hunter. You are keen of eye and swift of foot. Make yourself a bow and arrow. Go to the forests and hunt, and for every bird and animal that you bring back you will win a feather for your head-dress, and we shall call you Swift Arrow."

Little Nothing Yet smiled happily. He would

do it. He could do it. He knew the forests. He knew the haunts and habits of every bird and animal in the woodland. He left his father and went straight to his work. Before the full of the next moon his name would be Swift Arrow.

He searched for good, tough, elastic wood for his bow, and found it in the ash tree. He searched for a long tough slim root of an elm to serve as string for his bow. He worked hard and diligently for many days, and was very pleased with the results of his efforts. So was his father. He was very proud of Little Nothing Yet's bow and arrow, and showed it to every Indian in the encampment.

Strong Bow tested the weight of the arrow approvingly. "It is good! It is fine! It will be swift. You can get both bird and beast with this. Good hunting, Little Nothing Yet."

Little Nothing Yet cringed at the name, but he knew that it would not be long before the name was forgotten and until he would be known as Swift Arrow.

The next day he set out with the dawn. He went to the deep lake in the forest, and there he saw a fine wild goose preening her feathers. He raised

his bow. But the goose looked up at him beseech-
ingly, and said:

> *"Please don't shoot me, little Indian,*
> *I have little goslings at home;*
> *They are nesting in the rushes,*
> *I don't want to leave them alone."*

Little Nothing Yet lowered his bow. "I won't
shoot you, Mrs. Goose," he said. "You are safe from
my arrow."

"Thank you, little Indian. You are good," said
the goose as she flew toward the rushes and her
babies.

"She would have been a feather in my cap," said
the little boy to himself, "but I could not shoot her."
He walked along the shore and into the deep forest.
He met a little rabbit, a perky little cotton-tail, full
of the joy of living! Before Little Nothing Yet could
raise his bow the little rabbit spoke to him:

> *"Good morning! Good morning!*
> *I'm happy to see you.*
> *Good morning! Good morning!*
> *It is a nice day.*

You are a nice Indian
In your strong white buckskin;
I'm happy to meet you,
Will you be my friend?"

Little Nothing Yet nodded his head. "Yes,
little rabbit," he said, not even taking his arrow from
its sheath, "I'll be your friend. I'll play with you
some day, but I haven't time just now. I'm very, very
busy. I'm hunting."

"What for?" asked the little rabbit, wiggling
his little pink nose.

"For feathers for my cap," laughed Little
Nothing Yet. He couldn't help laughing. The
rabbit's wiggly nose was funny.

"The scarlet tanager might give you a feather,"
said the rabbit, "or the bluebird. They have beautiful feathers. If I wore feathers I'd give you one, but
I haven't any," laughed the bunny as he hopped on
his merry way.

The little Indian plunged forward. He could hear
a squirrel chattering in the clearing up ahead. He
pulled his arrow once more from his sheath. "He'll
be one feather in my cap. I'll get the squirrel." The

85

squirrel looked at him in a most friendly manner and
beckoned as he sang:

> *"Just look here. Just look here.*
> *See what I've found, all on the ground.*
> *There's hazel-nuts, acorns galore,*
> *And ripe brown chestnuts by the score.*
> *I'm gathering them for my winter store.*
> *Just look around."*

Little Nothing Yet looked at the busy little
squirrel. He nodded. "They are lovely nuts
and acorns," he said. "Where are you storing
them?"

"In the hollow tree," said the squirrel. "I
found a beautiful hollow tree with a deep, deep
hollow. I shan't be hungry this winter. Winter's long
and cold, you know, and a little squirrel can get very
hungry if the deep snow comes and covers the nuts on
the ground. But this winter I'll have plenty. I'll
have enough to share with you if you should run out
of food, little Indian."

"Thank you," said the little boy. "That is very
kind of you. But my father, the great chief, also

stores food for the winter. He will feed me when the deep snows come."

The little squirrel cocked her head to one side and then to the other. "That is very nice," she said. "I have no one to look after me, but I don't mind. I'm happy. It is such a lovely world, isn't it? It's so good to be alive in the sunlight, don't you think?"

Once more Little Nothing Yet put his arrow into its sheath. He couldn't use his arrow on a squirrel who loved life in the sunlight. He said good-bye and went on his way. He came to a woodland stream, and to his surprise and delight he saw a little brown bear getting a drink from its tumbling waters. If he could take a bear to his father's teepee on his first day of hunting, he would be the envy of all at the encampment. He was drawing his bow when the little bear turned to face him. To his amazement, the little bear was crying. When he saw Little Nothing Yet he brushed aside his tears, and said hopefully, "Will you, please, help me, little Indian? I am lost. I have been lost since sun-up. I'm a wicked little bear. My mother told me not to run away, but I did. And now I'm lost. I want my mama."

Little Nothing Yet bit his own lip to keep from crying. He couldn't use his arrow on this little lost bear. He nodded his head and stroked the cub kindly. "I'll help you find your mama," he said. "I'll help you. Don't cry."

Little Nothing Yet looked north, south, east and west, wondering in which direction to search for the cub's mother.

A bluebird in a pine-tree sang:

"His mother's gone over the hilltop
She's looking for her little bear.
If you take him over the hilltop
You'll find that his mother is there."

Little Nothing Yet thanked the bluebird, and took the little bear up the hill and over and down. The worried mother bear was very happy to see her lost cub. Little Nothing Yet sighed as he watched them waddle away. "It's just no use," he said; "my bow is strong, my arrow is swift, but I am not a hunter."

He sat down by the river, and he sat and he sat until the evening star came into the sky. Slowly then, and shamefacedly, he went back to the teepee of his father.

"You have been gone many hours, my son," the great chief said. "The hunting must have been good."

Little Nothing Yet nodded. "It was good, my father," he said. "But I did not make a name for myself. I shall have no feathers in my cap. The wild goose had little goslings in the rushes. If I had pierced her with my arrow, her little ones would have been alone. The rabbit was very happy. He wanted me to be his friend in this lovely sun-lit world. The squirrel was very busy. She was storing acorns and nuts for winter. She said she would have enough for me were I hungry when the snows came. And I met a little bear, my father; but he was lost, and I took him to his mother. I have brought no game home with me. I am still 'Little Nothing Yet'."

The great chief smiled and shook his head. "You are not, my son. You have made a name for yourself today. You have kindness in your heart for all living things. You set out to become Little Swift Arrow. You have come home Little Good Arrow.

Would 'Good Arrow' please you as a name?"

The next day Little Good Arrow wore a six-feathered bonnet. One for the wild goose, one for the rabbit, one for the squirrel, one for the bluebird and two for the brown bears that he didn't bring home.

SCRAPPER

A little brown dog barked and ran excitedly down the street. A gray pigeon flew hurriedly to a church steeple. A little red squirrel scampered up a tree trunk, and was soon lost in the heavy foliage of the maple. A little girl viewed the scene with wonder and cautiously stepped into a doorway. Something was going to happen! It was clear to her that the little brown dog, the gray pigeon and the red squirrel had scuttled to safety fearing some approaching danger. The little girl waited. A kitten rounded the corner. A pretty little fluffy black kitten with eyes that matched the new green of spring-time. He walked softly on padded feet, his head and tail held high. The little girl laughed merrily as she stepped back to the sidewalk.

"But they can't be frightened of you," she said. She went forward to meet the kitten and, as she reached him, she bent to stroke his soft black coat. "Hello, you pretty little kitten," she said. "You are very sweet, did you know that?"

His back hunched and his fur stood on end like a million flaming needles. Claws appeared from behind the black velvet cushions on which he walked and he snarled, "Yioew . . . Yioew."

The little girl pulled her hand away quickly and backed into a nearby hedge. The kitten went his proud angry way. The little girl gasped in amazement. "It was you!" she gasped. "The dog and the pigeon and the squirrel are afraid of you."

The kitten crossed the street and went into the neighboring park, and disappeared behind a clump of blue spruce. The little girl shook her head. "I just can't believe it," she said. "How can a pretty little kitten like that frighten the dogs and birds and the squirrels? It's very strange."

She went into the neighborhood grocery store, to which she had set out on an errand for her mother. She knew the grocer well. They were old friends. "Mr. Poppety," she said. "I just saw the funniest thing. I was coming to your store when, all of a sudden, a little brown dog ran away, a pigeon spread her wings and flew to the church steeple and the little red squirrel on Mr. McTavish's lawn scampered up the maple-tree like a flash. I knew they were frightened. And then, what do you suppose? A tiny little black kitten came round the corner."

Mr. Poppety burst out laughing. "That would be Scrapper," he said.

"You know the little kitten, sir?" said the little girl.

"I know him well, Katy," said Mr. Poppety. "I've been chasing him out of my back shop for weeks. I took the broom to him the other day."

"Why?" asked Katy.

"I don't know why. Just because he came into my back shop, I guess," said the storekeeper.

"Perhaps he was hungry," said Katy.

"Perhaps he was, but I have no time for hungry cats. I've enough to do to look after my customers," said Mr. Poppety.

Katy's face saddened, and Mr. Poppety, in spite of himself, hurried to defend his action. "Mr. Beasly, down at the fishmarket, had the same trouble," he said. "He told me that he'd put the scrapings of the fish he'd cleaned out in the garbage can. The garbage man came to take them away, and there, bold as you please in the garbage can, was Mr. Kitten. He snarled at the garbage man and scratched him. Mr. Beasly heard the garbage man say, 'You're quite a scrapper, aren't you?' We've called him 'Scrapper' ever since."

Katy nodded. "It's not a very nice name for such a pretty little kitten," she said. "Who owns him?"

Mr. Poppety shrugged his shoulders. "Nobody as far as I know," he said. "He's just a homeless waif. I think he may live at the docks. I saw him one day

94

when I took a load of groceries down to a freighter."

Katy pondered. "Poor little Scrapper," she said with great understanding. "I don't suppose anyone has ever been kind to him in his whole life. I think that's why he fights and frightens other little animals. I think he thinks the whole world is against him, and he's trying to fight his way alone."

Mr. Poppety scratched his chin and looked down at the little girl on the other side of the counter. "That sounds very wise for so small a girl," he said.

"It isn't really," said Katy. "It's just that I was thinking that if I were hungry and was looking for food and someone took the broom to me, or if I'd found some food and someone snatched it away from me, I'd probably fight, too. I don't know for sure, but I think I would. I've never had to fight, of course, because my mother and father are good to me. I'm sorry for Scrapper. Good-bye, Mr. Poppety."

Katy took her parcel and went slowly down the street. She was wondering where Scrapper had gone. Where was he now?

He was sitting on a breakwater down at the pier. Tears were flowing from his green eyes and splashing

on the rocks below. A water-rat saw them. "That's
funny," he said to himself. "It can't be raining.
There's not a cloud in the sky." He clambered up
the stone wall and saw the weeping kitten. His first
impulse was to laugh. It was funny to see Scrapper
crying. He realized suddenly that his little friend
was unhappy. "What's the matter, Scrapper?" he
asked.

"Don't call me 'Scrapper'," sobbed the kitten.

"It's your name, isn't it?" said the water-rat.
"It's been your name as long as I've known you."

"It's not my name. It's just what everybody
calls me," said Scrapper.

The water-rat raised his skimpy eyebrows. "I
guess you've earned the name for yourself. You're
always scrapping, aren't you?"

Scrapper nodded. "Yes," he said, "but I don't
want to. It's just that . . . well, nobody likes me,
Water-rat."

"Did you ever give them a chance to like you?"
asked the rat.

"I don't know," sobbed Scrapper. "Everywhere I go people chase me away. Scat! they say.
Scat! Scat! I made up my mind I'd say 'SCAT'

right back at everybody. But it doesn't help any, Water-rat. It doesn't help at all."

"It certainly isn't the golden rule," said the rat. Seeing the bewildered look on the sad little face of the kitten, he explained himself. "The golden rule is 'always do to others as you would like them to do to you'! But, of course, you've had no one to tell you these things. A little pretty kitten like you should have a nice home and friends. Did something happen today to make you cry?"

Scrapper nodded. "Yes," he said. "A little girl! I met a little girl. She stopped and bent to stroke my fur. She said I was very pretty and very sweet, and, Water-rat, I showed my claws and yowled at her. She looked so surprised that she backed into the hedge. Water-rat, her voice was soft and gentle. Do you think she meant what she said?"

"Yes, I do," said the rat. "Yes, I believe she did. That's just what you need, Scrapper. A little girl! She'd be kind to you, and you wouldn't have to scrounge any more, and no one would say 'Scat' at you or chase you with a broom. Do you know where she lives?"

Scrapper shook his head. "I don't know exactly," he said. "I'd not seen her before, but she must live somewhere near Mr. Poppety's grocery store. That's where she was going."

"We'll find her," said the water-rat. He laughed at the look on Scrapper's face. "Oh, I don't mean I'll find her. No one wants a water-rat on his premises. I know my place, and I know enough to stay in it. But we'll get the little brown dog to find her. He often comes down here to watch the gulls. I'll explain the whole situation to him. He's a nice little dog. He'll understand and forgive."

The little brown dog did. He said he would begin his search for the little girl that very afternoon, and that very afternoon he heard a little girl singing:

"I met a little cat today,
I thought him very sweet.
His eyes were green, his coat was black,
He had four velvet feet.
But when I stopped to speak to him,
He snarled and ran away;
I'm sorry for the little cat,
The cat I met today.

98

"I wondered why he acted so
And why he snarled at me;
I went into the grocery store,
Told Mr. Poppety.
And Mr. Poppety said that
The kitten had no home,
That everyone chased him away,
And that he lived alone.

"The little cat needs someone to
Be kind to him and good.
To play with him, and give him milk
And lots of nice warm food.
I wish he were my little cat,
I wish that he were mine;
We'd play together in the sun
And have fun all the time."

The little dog barked joyously. He had found
Scrapper's little girl. There was no doubt of that.
She had been singing about Scrapper. He went
toward her and barked. He was trying to get her to
follow him, but the little girl did not understand
what he wanted. How could he MAKE her under-

stand? Then he had an idea. Propped up against a tree near where she sat on the lawn was a doll. It was a dangerous idea, but it was the best the little brown dog could think of at the moment. He leapt forward, seized the doll in his mouth and ran off with it.

"Come back, come back here, you bad little dog," cried Katy, running at top speed after the little brown dog. "Drop my doll. Drop her, I say," she begged as she rounded the corner.

But the little brown dog had no intention of dropping the doll. He was taking the doll to the wharf, where Scrapper, the unhappy kitten, sat waiting. He was not running at his top speed. He knew that Katy could not keep up with him if he did. He ran at an easy canter, keeping far enough ahead of her to avoid her catching up with him.

The water-rat saw him coming. "He's done it, Scrapper. The little girl is coming. I'll duck out of the way. She might be frightened of me. I am an ugly-looking creature."

The little brown dog dropped the doll at Scrapper's feet. "This is your chance, Scrapper," he said. "Be as nice as you know how to be."

A puffing Katy reached the breakwater. She saw her doll, none the worse for wear, and she saw the kitten. "Oh," she squealed in delight. "It's Scrapper."

She turned to the little brown dog. "You brought me down here on purpose, didn't you, little dog? You brought me down to see Scrapper. But, Scrapper, I'm sort of afraid of you. You tried to scratch me this morning."

"Yieow," said Scrapper. "Yieow."

"You're sorry, aren't you?" said Katy.

"Yieow," said Scrapper sadly.

"You want to go home and live with me, don't you?" said Katy.

"Mieow . . . mieow . . . mieow," cried Scrapper eagerly.

The little brown dog lost no time in spreading the good news. The grey pigeon pecked happily for seeds. The red squirrel gamboled on the green lawn, and the little brown dog knew his black nose was safe for ever from Scrapper's claws.

Two days later Katy went into Mr. Poppety's store on another errand for her mother. His eyes went poppety when he saw the kitten in her arms.

"Katy," he said, "that's Scrapper, isn't it?"

"No," said Katy. "It WAS Scrapper, but now he's 'Sweetie Pie'. Would you, please, give me a pound of tea and a package of rice, Mr. Poppety."

"Sweetie Pie!" repeated the storekeeper. "Sweetie Pie! I just can't believe it." Mr. Poppety laughed. So did the water-rat when he heard it.

FIVE AND ONE

Penny looked at the birthday cake on the kitchen table. It was the most beautiful thing she had ever seen. It had been made especially for her. Penny put her nose dangerously near the thick white icing that completely covered the big round cake. It smelled of almond. Penny loved almond flavoring. She then turned her attention to the little pink rosebuds that were nestled in pale green sugar leaves. Although Penny had seen her mother make the rosebuds by squeezing the pink and green icing through a paper funnel, she was now convinced that the flowers had grown there. And there was her name, too, "Penny Pink", written on the cake in green frosting. She had saved the candles for the last. The candles were her pride and joy. There were six. Five white ones, which made a perfect ring as they circled the beautiful cake, and one pink one standing in the centre in the heart of a rose.

"One, two, three, four, five," she said as she counted the white candles. "And one pink one makes six. Five and one are six, and that is what I am. Six."

It was a beautiful age to be. No one could call her "baby" again. Penny remembered when she was four and went to nursery school. It had been very nice, but her mother had always called to bring her home. Five had been a little better. She had gone to kindergarten and had learned many things, and on fine days had come home alone. But now that she was six she would go to school. Real school, where seven-, eight-, nine-, ten-, eleven-year-olds went! Yes, six was the nicest age to be. It was growing up. Penny counted the candles again to be sure. "One, two, three, four, five white, and one pink made six." Penny was having a birthday party. She would count the candles again when her guests came, so that everyone would know that she was six.

"Penny," called her mother from upstairs. "Penny, it's time you had your bath, dear. I've laid out your party dress and socks and underthings. Come along."

"Yes, Mum," called Penny. She didn't want to leave that cake with five and one candles, but she knew that she must. She ran upstairs to her room. There was another surprise waiting for her. The party dress. Penny had expected to wear her blue-and-white dotted organdy, but there was a fluffy pink dress spread out on the bed. It was made of shimmering silk and smocked in rosy shades. "Oh, Mum!" cried Penny. "It's beautiful. It matches the rosebuds on my beautiful cake."

Mrs. Pink nodded. "Yes, I thought a little girl named Penny Pink should have a pink dress on her sixth birthday."

Penny hopped about as she made ready for her bath, making up a song as she hopped:

> *"Once when I was very young*
> *I was small and I was one;*
> *And I grew and grew and grew*
> *Until I was two, two, two.*
> *Pretty soon I grew some more,*
> *I was three and I was four.*

> *"Then one day, oh! sakes alive!*
> *Had a birthday, I was five.*
> *Five was very nice to be;*
> *Better'n two and better'n three.*
> *But I'm six years old today,*
> *It's the very best I say."*

Mrs. Pink laughed merrily at the gay little song, and sat down on the big easy chair in Penny's room. Penny frowned. "Mum," she said, "you're not going to stay there, are you?"

"Yes," replied Mrs. Pink. "I'm going to stay here and wait until you've bathed. Then I'm going to button your dress for you. Even if you were seven today, you'd need someone to help you button the dress. Anyone who has a dress that buttons at the back needs a little help."

"But, Mum," said Penny. "Couldn't you wait in the kitchen? I don't like leaving my five-and-one birthday cake alone. Something might happen to it."

Mrs. Pink laughed again. "What could possibly happen to your five-and-one cake? Has anything serious ever happened to anything in our kitchen?"

Mrs. Pink did not know that this was the day something serious WAS going to happen to something in her kitchen. Mrs. Pink did not know that Matilda Mouse was having a birthday, too, in the jam closet in the cellar. If Mrs. Pink had known she would not have rested so easily in the big flowered chair by the window.

Matilda was not happy on her birthday, however. She was crying, and her friend Milton was desperate. Nothing he could say seemed to quieten her. "But, Tildy," he said, "I did the best I could. I don't like to say this, but I risked my life, Tildy, going to the bake shop to get this lovely chocolate cupcake for a birthday cake."

Matilda stamped her foot angrily. "Don't call

me 'Tildy'. My name is 'Matilda', and who asked you to risk your life? I didn't, but if you were going to be brave enough to do it, why didn't you get a candle for the cake at the same time?"

Milton gulped. Tildy did not seem to be impressed by the great risk he had taken to get her the chocolate cupcake. He had not told her that he narrowly missed getting swatted by the baker's rolling-pin as he ran from the counter with the cake. And now she wanted a candle!

"Well," she persisted. "What about it?"

"What about what?" asked the unhappy Milton.

"The candle," said Matilda. "Don't you understand? I want a candle for my cake."

Milton cringed under Matilda's glassy stare. He wanted her to have a happy birthday, but he had already risked his life once today. His luck might not hold. "I don't know where to get a candle," he said.

"I do," said Matilda. "Upstairs! I happen to know that Penny is having a birthday party today. If she's having a party she is sure to have a cake, and if she's having a cake it's up in the kitchen; and if you're as brave as you say you are you'll go up there right now and get a candle."

108

"But Penny may be there," said Milton.

Matilda sighed. "Have you no ears? Can't you hear the water running in the pipes? That means she's having a bath, and she doesn't have a bath in the kitchen. All you have to do is climb up the water-pipe and into the closet under the sink. Push the door open, go into the kitchen and get a candle."

Milton hesitated. Matilda shrugged her shoulders. "Don't go if you don't want to," she said. "Charlie Churchmouse is coming to my party. He'll go."

Milton needed no further urging. He leapt from the shelf in the jam closet and ran toward the water-pipe. He scampered up the pipe and squeezed his way into the sink closet. Fortunately for him, the door was not on the latch. He went into the kitchen. All was still. The faint flavor of almond helped him locate the cake on the table. He jumped toward it. He could not help squeaking in delight. The cake was the most beautiful thing he had ever seen. He and Penny were in agreement on that. He backed up to the edge of the table and leapt to the cake. His feet sank into the soft white frosting. The white candles made a picket-fence around him.

109

He saw the one pink candle in the centre. He would take that one to Tildy, rose and all. If she were not pleased with it, he would give up. It took all his strength to loosen the candle from the cake, but he managed to do so. He pushed it to the table, to the floor, and then rolled it toward the sink closet. He ran into some difficulty. Pots and pans which were stacked neatly inside the closet had been no trouble to him on his way out. He had jumped over them, but to pull the candle up over them to the hole in the floor was difficult. He tried it. A pan tumbled and rolled across the kitchen.

Penny, who had finished her bath, heard the noise and looked at her mother anxiously. "Do you think it's my cake? Do you think the cake has fallen?"

"I don't see how it could have, dear," her mother laughed, "but you won't be satisfied until you find out. Go and see."

Penny's mouth flew open in dismay when she saw the beautiful cake. She could not believe her eyes. One candle was gone. "One, two, three, four, five. But I'm six! There has to be six candles. The pink one is gone." She bent over the cake and saw the tiny tracks Milton had left in the frosting. "A mouse!" she gasped. The now terrified Milton made a mighty effort to pull the candle through the hole by the water-pipe. Another pan rolled. Penny ran to the sink closet. She saw the struggling Milton. It was easy enough to catch him because he was determined to take the pink candle with him.

Penny picked him up by the tail. "You wicked little mouse," she sobbed, looking into Milton's beady and fear-filled eyes. "You've spoiled my birthday cake. You took my pink candle. I don't know what to do to you. You've ruined my party."

The fear in Milton's eyes changed to tears. "I'm sorry," he said. "I didn't mean to spoil your cake. I took just one candle. You have five left."

"Can't you understand?" said Penny. "I am six today. Six! I had five white and one pink to make six. And now my cake is ruined."

Milton tried to free himself from Penny's hold. "Your cake is still alright, isn't it?"

"No," said Penny. "We couldn't eat a cake that a mouse had walked on."

"Why?" asked Milton. "Why?"

"Because," sobbed Penny. "That's why. And

111

you needn't struggle that way. I'm not going to let you go. Why did you have to spoil my day? I was so happy."

Matilda, who had heard all, came up the hole by the water-pipe. It was all her fault. Had she been satisfied with her own cake, Milton would not now be dangling in the hands of the enemy. Had she been satisfied, Penny would have had a happy birthday. She spoke out: "Please let him go, Penny," she pleaded. "It is not his fault. It is mine. I asked him to risk his life to get me a candle for MY cake. Milton didn't want to come. Really he didn't. This is my birthday, too."

"Your birthday," said Penny, so taken by surprise that she almost dropped the trembling mouse in her hand. "Who are you?"

"I am Matilda," said the little mouse, dropping her eyelids in shame. "I am having my birthday party in the jam closet. Charlie Churchmouse is coming, and Dolly Deermouse, and Fitzgerald Fieldmouse, and many others. Now my party is spoiled, too. You aren't going to let Milton go, are you?"

Penny cocked her head to one side. She looked at the frightened Milton and the pleading little Matilda.

112

"I'll let him go if you invite me and my friends to your party in the jam closet. I have no birthday cake to give them now, but I have ice-cream and candy and sandwiches. They might be satisfied with them if I told them that they could go to a mouse's party. Well, what do you say?"

Matilda nodded. Matilda agreed. At that moment Matilda would have promised anything to save her little friend. Penny released Milton and, more than that, she pushed the pink candle down the hole for him. Then she dashed upstairs to tell her mother what had happened.

"It is too bad about the cake, Penny, but if you are happy about the situation, it's alright with me," said mother. "It's your birthday."

Penny's guests were delighted with the idea of going to a mouse's party. They were amazed when they saw the charming little apartment in the jam closet. Matilda had done wonders with the place. The chocolate cupcake, with the pink candle in the centre, sat on a pretty little table which had been made from a chocolate box. Tildy even had a music-box, and all the mice danced together for Penny and her friends.

While they twirled about on their toes, Matilda sang:

"I want to thank Penny
For being so kind, 'cause
She let Milton go when I begged for his sake.
I'm sorry, so sorry, I sent him upstairs, 'cause
I did not know then he would ruin her cake.
I wanted a candle,
A pretty, pink candle,
'Cause it was my birthday I wanted one so.
But never again will I risk a good friend
For so selfish a reason.
I'm wicked I know."

Milton went to Matilda. "No, Tildy, no," he said.
"Yes, Milton, yes," said Penny. "She was selfish.
But I think she has learned a lesson. And even if I
didn't have my birthday cake, I'm still six. I'm still
five and one."

Penny's friends agreed that Penny's sixth birthday was the most exciting day they had ever had.
Penny thought so, too.

114

CARNIVAL KITTY CAT

Kitty Cat didn't know about carnivals until the day he fell right into the middle of one. Kitty Cat had been walking along the road when, without warning, the sky darkened. Rain fell in torrents, and the wind which followed swept Kitty Cat off his feet and carried him swirling through the sky. The little cat mewed in fear, and tried in vain to clutch at the branches of the swaying trees. Up and down and around about he was whirled. He closed his eyes, thinking that his end had come. Suddenly he was plucked from his unhappy plight through the air. Something had reached out for him and had curled about him like a thick warm blanket. His little heart was pounding with new fear. Slowly he opened his eyes and looked into the face of an elephant. Kitty Cat had never seen an elephant before.

The big animal understood and said kindly, "Do not be frightened, little cat. I'll keep you safe until the storm blows over."

"Thank you very much," said Kitty Cat, "but how did you pick me out of the sky?"

"With my trunk," said the big gray animal. "I'm an elephant, you know."

"No, I didn't know," said Kitty Cat. "I don't know much of anything. I'm such a little Kitty Cat. I have seen dogs and squirrels and chipmunks and rabbits, but up until now I've never seen an elephant."

"That's not surprising," said Kitty Cat's new friend. "Elephants do not run about freely like dogs and squirrels. In this country you'll find us in zoos and carnivals and circuses. I'm in a carnival."

"I don't know about carnivals, either," said the little cat.

The elephant did her best to explain life in a carnival to Kitty Cat. She told him of the men on the flying trapeze, of the prancing ponies, of the camels and giraffes, of bareback riders and performing seals, of the delicious aroma of roasting peanuts and honied popcorn, and of the Merry-go-round. "Of course I've never had a ride on the Merry-go-round," she added laughingly. "I'm too big for a Merry-go-round."

"You are big," said Kitty Cat, "but I'm glad you are. If you'd been small you wouldn't have been able to catch me when I went flying past you. And, Mrs. Elephant, I'm ever so grateful to you."

The elephant was pleased. She liked the little cat. "I'll set you down, Kitty Cat," she said. "I think the storm is about over. Where are you going now?"

Tears welled up in the little cat's green eyes. "I don't know where I'm going, because I don't know where I came from," he said. "I was living in a barn, and I went out to take a walk. The wind picked me up and carried me away, and now I don't know where I am."

"You're with me," laughed the elephant, "and if you'd like to stay with me and travel in my van, I'd like to have you."

Kitty Cat purred happily as he nodded his little grey head. The matter was settled. Kitty Cat joined the show.

The storm ended as quickly as it had begun and the carnival came to life again. The music of the Merry-go-round began to blare. The vendors began to cry out their wares, and the people who had run for shelter during the rain began to mill about again. Kitty Cat pricked up his ears to listen to the unfamiliar sounds of the carnival.

"Go along the midway and take a look," said the elephant. "Come back here later and see my act. You'll know my tent. It has my picture on the outside." The big animal hung her head as if embarrassed at what she was about to say. "They say I give a fine performance. The children love me."

The happy little cat left his big new friend and followed the sounds to the midway. He looked along the lane of coloured lights and flying banners and wondered if he were dreaming. As he moved forward he found himself in a forest of tramping feet. It was not a safe place for a little kitten to be. He managed to work his way out of the crowd, and he found a tree. From his perch on a low-lying branch he viewed the new world that he had discovered. Ferris Wheels were spinning, Merry-go-rounds were whirling. The giant Caterpillar was wiggling over its steel rails. Screams of laughter came from the Roller Coaster as its merry passengers dipped and dived on their strange journey of ups-and-downs. Kitty Cat was fascinated. "They say that a cat has nine lives," he said to himself. "I'm glad. I'd never be able to see all of the carnival in one life."

It was several hours before he returned to Mrs. Elephant. More surprises awaited him. A complete change had come over the elephant. She was shining gold. Kitty Cat gasped. "They gild me for the show, Kitty Cat," explained the elephant. "I'm called 'Goldie' in the ring."

"You're beautiful, Goldie," said the little cat.

"Thank you," said the elephant. "Kitty Cat, I spoke to Cook about you. He has some milk and

119

bacon scraps for you. Go over to the cookhouse and have your supper, then come to the big tent and see me perform."

The cook was very friendly. He set a dish of fresh milk on the ground for Kitty Cat. The bacon scraps were delicious. "I hear you're joining the Carnival, Kitty Cat," the cook said.

"Yes, sir," said Kitty Cat. "I'm going to travel with Goldie. I'm going to see her act tonight."

"You'll be proud of her," said the cook. "She's nothing short of great."

Kitty Cat was proud of Goldie. His tiny heart pounded with pride when he heard the ring-master call out, "Ladies and gentlemen, we bring you that mighty, that magnificent, that marvellous beast of the jungle, Goldie the Elephant."

Goldie danced. Goldie stood on her golden head. Goldie walked through a monstrous hoop of fire. Goldie stepped over her trainer with ease and grace. Goldie bowed and left the ring. The audience cheered and cheered.

The next morning the show moved on. Kitty Cat was very happy in the big red van that carried Goldie. When the carnival set up in the next town

Kitty Cat felt he really belonged. He had a sudden urge to be a performer.

Goldie shook her great head when Kitty Cat told her this. "No, Kitty Cat," she said, "you can't be a performer. Don't you understand? You must have an unusual act to be a performer. A little untrained barn cat cannot be part of the show."

"I can climb trees," said Kitty Cat. "Isn't that unusual?"

"Any little cat can climb trees," said Goldie kindly. "Just forget about being in the carnival. Be happy to be with it."

But Kitty Cat couldn't forget. He thought and thought of some unusual thing that he might do. He wanted to hear the children cheer for him. He walked along the midway, hoping that he might get an idea. But none came. He reached the Merry-go-round. It was just about to start. The man at the Merry-go-round knew Kitty Cat. "Hello!" he said. "Do you want a ride? There's an empty horse."

Without waiting for Kitty Cat's reply, the man lifted the little cat to the saddle of a blue horse, and away they went.

Kitty Cat had difficulty in staying on the whirling

horse. The saddle was highly polished, and Kitty Cat's claws could not get a grip on its shining surface. He took a flying leap into the air and landed on a balloon that had fallen from the hands of a little girl. The balloon began to roll like a ball. Kitty Cat managed to stay on the top of it, balancing himself as he rolled along. And then one of his claws burst the balloon. The little girl cried out in dismay. The little cat cried out in delight. He had an idea. He ran to the balloon-man.

"Please, Mr. Balloon Man," he pleaded, "will you give me a balloon? I have no money but I have an idea, and if it is a good one you'll sell many balloons."

The balloon man obliged and, with the string of the bouncing red balloon in his mouth, Kitty Cat went to Goldie. He revealed his plan to the elephant. Goldie roared with laughter. "I think it's wonderful, Kitty Cat," she said. "We'll try it. Watch my act very carefully tonight, and just before I take my final bow roll the balloon into the ring."

"Yes," said Kitty Cat, "and thank you for helping me, Goldie."

Kitty Cat spent the rest of the afternoon

balancing himself on the balloon. He worked very carefully, knowing full well that if he should burst the precious bauble he would lose his chance of showing his skill. He cleaned himself until his fur was like shining grey velvet. He wished that he had some sort of costume to wear. "I'll go to Oriana," he said to himself. "She will keep my secret, and she knows all about costumes. She always looks so beautiful on the flying trapeze."

Oriana heard Kitty Cat through and shook her head. "I wouldn't advise a costume, Kitty Cat," she said. "You're not used to costumes. You'd find a costume awkward and you might fumble. I have a better idea." She opened a box on her dressing-table and took from it a bracelet of brilliants. She snapped it around Kitty Cat's neck. "How's that?" she asked. "Does it feel comfortable?"

"Yes," said Kitty Cat. "It feels comfortable and looks beautiful. Thank you, Oriana."

"Think nothing of it," laughed the pretty circus girl. "And good luck."

That night the tent was filled to the brimming. Goldie was met with the usual cheers and applause. Just as she was taking her final bow the audience saw a

123

little gray cat, wearing a brilliant choker and carrying a red balloon, enter the ring. They sat strangely quiet as they watched his progress. When he reached Goldie, the big elephant picked up the kitten and the balloon and set them carefully on her broad back. Kitty Cat mounted the balloon and rolled it up and down, balancing himself perfectly all the while. As a climax to his unusual act, Kitty Cat rolled the balloon out to the very tip of Goldie's trunk, which was now raised and waiting. With one quick movement he sank a claw into the flimsy bauble. It burst noisily. As the balloon collapsed Goldie rolled the little kitten in her trunk just as she had done the day of the storm. Swaying in his gray elephant hammock, Kitty Cat waved his gray paws at the cheering crowd.

The ring-master stood open-mouthed during the whole performance. The circus manager went to him. "Stop gaping and get down to business," he said. "We've a new act here. A wonderful act! Say something! Announce it!"

The bewildered ring-master went into action. "Ladies and Gentlemen," he called, "you have just witnessed the most unusual act of the century. You have seen tonight, Ladies and Gentlemen, for the first time in any circus, an elephant and a kitten work together with amazing skill and dexterity. Ladies and Gentlemen, meet Carnival Kitty."

As Goldie's van rolled through the night she said to her happy little companion, "I'm proud of you, Kitty Cat. I didn't think you could do it."

"I couldn't have done it alone, Goldie," said Kitty Cat. "You helped me. Oriana and the balloon man helped me." Kitty Cat laughed. "And the storm helped me, too. Yes, I think the storm helped me most of all. If it hadn't been for the storm, I'd never have been Carnival Kitty."

PETER'S MAGIC ROOM

Some people say it was all a dream. Some people say it was all pretend. But Peter says it is true, and Peter should know. It happened to Peter.

Peter was a little boy who liked the outdoors. In Spring he liked the opening buds and the rippling

streams and the birds who came back to sing of the
fresh new world. In Summer, he liked the drone of
the bumble-bee and the frilled bonnets of the daisies,
and the tall grasses, amongst which hid all sorts of
tiny living things. In Autumn, the falling leaves and
the frequent visits of Jack Frost were his delight.
But of all the seasons he liked Winter best, with its
snow and ice. Peter was up at the crack of dawn
every morning and was out to greet the day.

But one morning, and it being in winter, Peter
woke up looking like his mother's best polka-dot
apron. "Back to bed, young man," his mother
said when she saw him. "You have the chicken-
pox."

Peter viewed himself in the mirror. He nodded.
"But they don't hurt, Mum. The chicken-poxes, I
mean! I don't have to go to bed. I can take these
chicken's poxes out to skate, mayn't I?"

"You may not," said his mother. "For one
thing, it wouldn't be fair to the other children, and
for another thing, you might get cold. A cold and
chicken-pox are not a good combination. You'll
have to stay in bed two or three days at least."

"Two or three days!" gasped Peter. "But,

Mum, I can't stay in two or three days. I'll smother without any fresh air."

Mrs. Peabody laughed. "I'll risk that," she said. "You might be surprised at what a pleasant time you'll have in your pretty bedroom. I don't believe you've ever taken time to look at the new wallpaper. It has dogs and kittens and ponies and beautiful geese on it."

"Hah," said Peter disdainfully. "The dogs can't bark. The kittens can't mew. The ponies can't neigh. The geese can't quack."

"B–E–D, bed for you, my Speckled Darling," said his mother firmly.

The outdoor man had to stay in the house. Almost grudgingly he began to investigate the new wallpaper. He had to admit that it was interesting. The little red-and-white horse above the window was a pinto. He was wearing a western saddle and blanket. "Pinto," Peter said, "I suppose that cowboy over by the drapes is going to ride you through the purple sage. But what's keeping him? Why doesn't he get on you and ride? Perhaps a little music would help him." Peter leaned across the bed full length and took a record from the cabinet. He put it on his

128

small record-player nearby, and began to compose a song that he hoped would urge the cowboy near the drapes to mount the pony above the window.

> *"Come on Cowboy ride*
> *On the pinto beside*
> *The window, 'cause I'd like to see*
> *The sage and the plain.*
> *Now I ask you again*
> *Come on, Cowboy, please ride for me.*
> *Ride, ride on the range.*
> *Please ride on that pony today,*
> *'Cause I am in bed, with my speckles so red*
> *And I can't go outdoors to play."*

But nothing happened. The cowboy didn't move. He didn't even wave his ten-gallon hat. And the pinto stood quietly staring at the green-paper grass at his feet.

Peter turned his attention to the little blue dog near the bookcase. "Bark, little dog, bark," said Peter. He whistled, but the blue dog seemed interested only in the paper bone at his feet. Peter sighed. Perhaps the yellow cat near the clothes-closet door might listen to him. The cat looked lively enough. In fact, it looked ready to pounce. Peter pondered. "I know what," he said to himself, "I'll make up a song about a mouse. It won't be true, of course, but when the cat comes looking for the mouse, I'll tell him the song is a joke, and I'll give him some of my milk. He should be satisfied with some nice fresh milk." Peter dropped the needle on the record again and sang:

> "One day in the house,
> I saw such a fat mouse.
> He was gray and as fat as could be,
> And I said 'hello', and I said 'do you know
> That I'd like you to come play with me?'
> And that little mouse
> And I played all over the house,
> And it could be today that he'd come here to
> play,
> That fat little gray little mouse."

Peter looked sharply at the yellow cat. But the cat didn't even as much as arch his back at the mention of a fat little gray little mouse.

"I give up," said Peter in disgust. "Nobody will talk to me."

There was a rustle above the head of his bed. "That's because you don't talk to the right people," said a voice behind him. Peter swung around. It was the gray goose on the wallpaper who was talking. She was flapping her wings as if she were going to take off any minute. Peter laughed. "I'm sorry, Goose," said Peter, "but I didn't think of talking to you. I thought you were stupid. When I do anything stupid people say, 'Oh, don't be a goose'."

The goose tossed her gray head indignantly. "It is they who are stupid," she said. "If they would take the trouble to read about geese they would discover that we are the most intelligent of birds, that we learn quickly, and that we are loyal. And now, if you'll excuse me, I'll be on my way."

She flew from the paper and headed for the open window. Peter was too quick for her. He reached up and caught her by one leg. "Just a minute, Goose," Peter said, "where do you think you're going?"

"I don't have to think where I'm going," said the goose; "I know where I'm going, and my name is Gloria."

Peter roared with laughter. "Gloria!" he repeated. "Who gave you a name like that?"

"Her Royal Highness, the Princess Marietta Marie Maureen of Maurenia," said the goose. "I go to see her every day. She waits for me in the castle garden."

Peter was amazed, but not so much so that he should release Gloria. "I didn't know you flew away every day," he said.

"How could you?" asked the goose. "You're never in your room. You wouldn't be here now if you didn't have the chicken-pox. I'm glad you're an outdoor boy. You don't interfere with my comings and goings."

Peter tightened his grip on the goose. "I'm going to interfere today," he said. "You're my goose. You came off my wallpaper, so you're mine. I'm not going to let you go unless you take me with you!"

Gloria struggled to free herself. She could not. "Alright," she said, not too graciously. "I'll take you. Her Royal Highness has often longed for someone of her own age with whom to play. Get on my back and we'll go to Maurenia."

132

Peter mounted the big gray goose, and they flew out through the open window, as if it were an ordinary everyday thing to do. In a matter of seconds Peter saw the turrets of a castle. It sat on a hilltop beside the sea, and looked for all the world like the castles in his Fairy-tale Books. Gloria called out, "Hold on tightly, Peter, I'm going down."

And down they went, and into a rose-garden. Her Royal Highness Marietta Marie Maureen was sitting on a low marble wall that circled the fountain. She was crying. Her pretty face was buried in a lacy handkerchief. Gloria waddled toward her. "What is the matter, Your Highness?" she asked.

Marietta looked up and threw her arms about the gray goose's neck. "Oh, Gloria," she said, "I am in such trouble. I have been very naughty. I took the keys of the royal vault, and I took my papa's royal crown from its golden box. I love papa's crown jewels. The diamonds and the emeralds and the rubies and pearls are so pretty. I am not supposed to touch His Majesty's Crown, but I did. I just wanted to play with it, and I put it on and I climbed down over the rocks to the seashore. Some gypsies saw me and they came along the shore, and they seized papa's crown and they ran away with it. What am I going to do?"

Gloria shook her head. "I'm so befuddled at the moment," she said, "I can't think." She turned to Peter. "Do you know what to do, Peter?"

Her Royal Highness noticed Peter for the first time. She looked at him in his pyjamas and chicken-pox, and she burst into laughter. In spite of her trouble, she couldn't help it. She'd never seen anything quite so funny.

Peter laughed, too. "I don't blame you, Your Highness, for laughing at me," he said, "but you'd look just as funny if you had the chicken-pox."

"I have had them," said Her Highness. "I had them last week. Those are probably mine that you're wearing now. Gloria probably carried mine home to you. I'm sorry, Peter."

"Oh, that's alright," said Peter. "If she hadn't brought me your chicken-pox, I'd never have known that she flew away every morning, and I'd never have met you. But we should be talking about the gypsies. Where are they?"

"They went off in their caravan," said the little princess. "I don't know in which direction they headed. I don't know what my Majestic Papa will do to me. He is now a King without a crown."

"We've got to find those gypsies," said Peter. He turned to the goose. "Gloria, you are going to fly with Her Royal Highness and me. From away up in the sky we should be able to see the caravan. We'll get the royal crown from them, or my name isn't Peter Peabody."

The little princess wasn't so sure. "But even if we see the caravan, Peter, we're no match for the gypsies," she said.

"We'll think of something," said Peter. "Climb aboard."

Marietta climbed on the broad back of the goose. Peter climbed up behind her. Gloria took to the air. Up, up, up she went, high above the castle, the trees and the church steeples. She circled over the landscape below. Peter cried out, "I see it. I see the caravan. That red speck down there on the winding road must be the caravan." Peter was in command of the situation. Peter suddenly knew just what to do. "Go down in front of the horses, Gloria. They'll have to stop the caravan if you fly in front of the horses."

Gloria plunged earthward, and fluttered directly in front of the horses' noses. They veered, and the gypsy pulled them to a stop. "What are you trying to do?" he shouted.

"We've come to get the royal crown," said Peter, keeping his face well hidden behind Marietta, "and we want it right now."

"You're brave, aren't you?" laughed the gypsy scornfully. "A very brave boy indeed, hiding behind a little girl! Two children and a goose! Do you think you're any match for the gypsies?"

"Yes, I do," said Peter, leaping from Gloria's back and running to the caravan. He put his foot on the step. "Either throw the crown to the road or I climb aboard, and you can see what I have."

"Chicken-pox!" gasped the gypsies inside the caravan. "He's got the chicken-pox. Don't let him in here. Give him the crown. Give him the crown, Togare. We don't want the chicken-pox."

Togare, the driver of the caravan, grumbled angrily as he tossed the crown to the soft shoulder of the road. "Take it," he said, "and get away from here. Get away, I tell you."

Gloria moved aside. The gypsy urged the horses

136

forward, and they went tearing down the road at a wild pace.

Marietta, Gloria and Peter laughed until they thought they would split their sides. "Who'd ever think the chicken-pox could save a royal crown?" said Peter.

It was his mother who answered him. "Did they?" she said.

Peter opened his eyes and sat up. "What are you doing here, Mum?"

"I brought your lunch," said Mrs. Peabody.

"Oh," said Peter, looking around him. "But where's Marietta? Where's Gloria?" He looked up at the wallpaper by the head of his bed. Gloria was home, too. He told his mother what had happened. She nodded, but he knew she didn't believe. Some people say he dreamed it. Some say it was just pretend. But Peter knows it to be true. Why shouldn't he? It happened to him!

WHAT HAPPENED IN
PUDDLEDUCK

Once upon a time, and long ago it was, too, the funniest thing happened in Puddleduck. Puddleduck was a village of comfortable homes and honest people. Everyone knew everyone else in Puddleduck, and everyone trusted everyone else in Puddleduck. There were six grocery stores, two general stores (that meant they kept everything), one toy shop, one ice-cream parlor and one policeman. They had no jail. They didn't need a jail. But the citizens of Puddleduck thought it gave the village distinction to have a policeman on the streets. He looked very handsome in his blue coat with the silver buttons, his blue trousers with their red stripe, his tall gray hat with its silver badge, and his long black boots which were so shiny they made the sun dance.

Besides decorating the streets of Puddleduck with his commanding figure, Sergeant Whistlestop looked after all the celebrations in the village. On Halloween he hung Jack-o'-Lanterns from the lamp-posts. On the twenty-fourth of May it was Sergeant Whistlestop who draped the town hall with bunting and who hoisted the flag. On Valentine's Day he hung red hearts on every door-knob. But the day dearest to Sergeant Whistlestop's heart was Christmas. He was for ever trying to think up some new way to make Puddleduck outstanding at that festive season.

"I just don't know," said Mrs. Fussybonnet to

139

Mrs. Plainhat, "what he can do this year to improve on last year. You'll remember he painted every door red and every fence green. Puddleduck looked just like a Christmas-card, and that's a fact."

"And the year before," said Mrs. Plainhat, "will you ever forget the year before? A snowman, wearing a holly wreath for a hat on every corner?"

Mrs. Fussybonnet nodded. "How the children did enjoy helping him with those snowmen! That's another thing about Sergeant Whistlestop. He's always thinking of the children. But that's the way with policemen. Children are their special care. But that year of the snowmen! My Willie came home every afternoon looking like a snowman himself. Do you remember the snowman at the corner of Petunia and Daffodil Lane? My Willie made the head of that snowman and, if I do say it myself, it was the best head in town. That snowman's face actually smiled."

Mrs. Plainhat remembered and agreed, but she was not going to waste her time talking about Willie Fussybonnet. She turned the conversation back to Sergeant Whistlestop. "And he's a one-man band, too. He certainly cheers up the evenings with that hand-organ of his. The way that man can make up songs."

While they were discussing him, the Sergeant passed by Mrs. Fussybonnet's house and he was calling, "Hear ye! Hear ye! All girls and boys quit your playing. Quit your noise. I want to meet you in the square at two o'clock. Will you be there? Hear ye! Hear ye!"

Mrs. Fussybonnet looked at Mrs. Plainhat and smiled. "He's up to something," she said. "He has a new idea and he's including the children, and I'll have all I can do to pry it out of Willie."

"Shame on you, Mrs. Fussybonnet," said Mrs. Plainhat. "You shouldn't pry into Christmas secrets."

"Well . . . uh . . . I figure that children should not have secrets from their parents," said Mrs. Fussybonnet defensively.

"I agree, with the exception of Christmas," said Mrs. Plainhat. "Everyone has Christmas secrets." She fastened her coat and started for the door. "I must be going along if I'm to get my plum-pudding steamed today."

At two o'clock the street was alive with children, and all running to the square to learn of

Sergeant Whistlestop's Christmas plans for Puddleduck. They gathered around the laughing policeman
while he sang:

> *"I thought it would be nice*
> *To have a Christmas-tree*
> *Standing in the square*
> *For everyone to see.*
> *We'll trim the tree with stars,*
> *With candles shining bright,*
> *And on the tree there'll be a gift*
> *For everyone that night.*
>
> *"On our tree there will be*
> *Christmas gifts for all;*
> *Hanging from the branches there'll*
> *Be presents great and small.*
> *Books and games, candy canes*
> *Dolls and velvet cats*
> *Choo-choo trains, weather vanes,*
> *Shoes and scarves and hats."*

The children cheered and roared with laughter,
and eagerly asked how they could help to bring about
this Christmas miracle.

"Well, now," said Sergeant Whistlestop, "the first thing we must do is choose a tree. We'll go to the woodland together. It's going to be quite a chore to find a tree big enough to hold all the gifts, and when we do find one big enough, it must be beautiful. It must be strong and green and well shaped. Shall we go to the woods?"

"Yes," thundered the children in approval. Their voices echoed up and down the streets, and mothers and fathers all over Puddleduck smiled. They knew that something exciting was being planned in the square, and they knew that their children were safe with Sergeant Whistlestop.

The Sergeant looked like the Pied Piper of Hamelin as he set out from the village, playing the hand-organ and followed by hundreds of children. The woods, sparkling with winter snow, were lovely that day. The chickadees chickadeed in wonder when they saw the policeman and the children. The squirrels chattered, but one little rabbit watched in silence. He wasn't going to wonder. He was going to find out what it was all about.

"Listen, everyone," said the Sergeant, "we'll spread out now to look for the tree, but no one must go beyond the sound of my voice. It's easy to get lost in the woods, and we don't want that to happen."

The children shook their heads. They would keep within the sound of his voice. Some of the children went in groups of threes. Some in twos! But little Jonathan Jellyred went alone. The inquisitive rabbit decided to follow him. Jonathan was so busy looking up at the giant trees that he didn't see the little cotton-tail at his feet. The rabbit knew that time was wasting, and he decided to make himself noticed. "Hey," he said sharply.

Jonathan Jellyred looked down and saw the fluffy little white fellow, who's pink-lined ears were twinkling with curiosity. "Hey yourself," laughed Jonathan, and sat down on a tree stump. "What's your name?"

"Henry. What's yours?"

"Jonathan," said Jonathan.

"It's a nice name," said Henry. "Jonathan, will you please tell me something? Why are all the children and Sergeant Whistlestop in the woods today?"

Jonathan's eyes widened. "Do you know Sergeant Whistlestop?" he said.

"Yes," said Henry. "I often go to the village. I like going to the village, especially to the park. There's a nice park in Puddleduck. I hide under the bandstand. But you didn't tell me why you were here."

Jonathan explained the situation to Henry. Told him how Sergeant Whistlestop had called them altogether and sang his song! Told him how on Christmas night there would be a Christmas-tree in the square with a present for everyone!

Henry nodded his head and leapt into the underbrush and disappeared. It was Willie Fussybonnet who found a suitable tree. Everyone agreed that the tree that Willie found was right in every way. It was cut down and dragged to the village. Henry watched it being taken away, from his hiding-place under the bramble bush. Henry was thinking. "It's such a nice idea. A present for every boy and girl in Puddleduck! It would be nice if every little rabbit in the woodland could have a Christmas present, too. What would a little rabbit like best for Christmas? Henry knew what he'd like best. A carrot! But he decided to

ask the others. He got one answer from everyone.
A carrot! Henry decided then and there to be the
rabbits' "Sergeant Whistlestop". He called them all
together and he sang:

"I thought it would be nice
To have a Christmas-tree
Standing in the park
For all of you and me
I'll trim the tree for you,
With carrots big and small.
On Christmas night there'll be carrots
For me and for you all.

"On our tree there will be
Carrots, carrots sweet.
Hanging on the branches there'll
Be carrots for a treat.
Carrots good . . . carrots fine,
They are hard to beat.
Merry Christmas for us all
With a carrot sweet."

The rabbits were delighted with the idea, and
told Henry they'd meet him in the park on Christmas

night. "But, Henry," said one little cotton-tail, "where are you going to get all the carrots?"

"Just leave that to me," said Henry.

Two days later Mrs. Plainhat went to the grocery store for carrots. "Yes, ma'am," said the storekeeper, and went to his back shop. There were no carrots. He scratched his head. "That's funny," he said, "I don't remember selling all my carrots."

Mrs. Plainhat went to the next store. No carrots! "Sorry, Mrs. Plainhat," the shopkeeper said, "I thought I had carrots. I can't remember selling them either; that's funny!"

Mrs. Plainhat went to the four other grocery stores (you remember there were six in Puddleduck). When Mrs. Plainhat announced that there wasn't a carrot in town, the people became suspicious, and a meeting was called.

"You'll have to investigate this carrot robbery, Sergeant Whistlestop," said the Mayor. "I know you're busy with the Christmas-tree. (It's no secret, you know. Willie Fussybonnet's mother pried it out of him.) We all know what you're planning and we like it, but you'll have to leave the tree to the children and end this carrot crime-wave."

147

Sergeant Whistlestop investigated all day, and found no clues. He investigated all night, and found no clues. But just at dawn, when he was walking through the park, he tripped over a carrot. Could the carrots be stored under the bandstand, in the place which was used to house the music-stands and the chairs? He looked. Carrots and carrots and carrots! Hundreds of carrots, all stacked in neat piles! The next morning he reported his findings to the Mayor. "But who is the thief?" asked the Mayor.

"I don't know that," said the policeman, "but the carrots are hidden there for a reason. The thief will give himself away. Something will happen."

The something happened on Christmas Eve. It was Jonathan Jellyred who noticed it first. "Mum, Mum," he called to his mother. "Look! Look toward the park. There are hundreds of chickadees over there and each one has something in his mouth."

Jonathan and his mother ran to the park, and all the other people in Puddleduck saw them running, and they ran, too. They couldn't believe their eyes. The chickadees were trimming the big spruce tree in the middle of the park with carrots. And the

148

carrots hung like golden baubles in the winter sunlight. And then the rabbits came marching from the woodland, led by Henry Cotton-tail, who was singing:

"We're going to have a merry time today,
  Because we have a Christmas-tree, so gay,
  The chickadees have trimmed our tree
  With carrots fine, for you and me,
  And we'll all have fun and carrots on Christmas
    Day."

Sergeant Whistlestop knew his duty, and he said to the six storekeepers, "Do you wish that I should seize the tree?"

"No," they laughed. "Rabbits don't know right from wrong. They didn't know they were stealing. Let them have their fun. But how on earth did they ever think of a tree?"

"I know," said Jonathan. "It's really Sergeant Whistlestop's idea. I told Henry about our tree the day I was in the woodland, and about how we were all going to get gifts. The carrot-tree is lovely, isn't it?"

"Beautiful," said Mrs. Fussybonnet, "and to

149

think we have the only one in the world. We'll become famous."

And they did. Puddleduck was put on the map; and it's there to this day, and all because of a policeman and a carrot-tree. The funniest things happened in the once upon a time.